ALICE SHARPE

THE BABY'S BODYGUARD

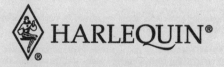

This book is dedicated to the memory of my mother with eternal gratitude for all the years of her love and support.

PLEASE RECYCLE • THIS PRODUCT IS RECYCLABLE

Recycling programs
for this product may
not exist in your area.

ISBN-13: 978-0-373-69476-1

THE BABY'S BODYGUARD

Copyright © 2010 by Alice Sharpe

ABOUT THE AUTHOR

Alice Sharpe met her husband-to-be on a cold, foggy beach in Northern California. One year later they were married. Their union has survived the rearing of two children, a handful of earthquakes registering over 6.5, numerous cats and a few special dogs, the latest of which is a yellow Lab named Annie Rose. Alice and her husband now live in a small rural town in Oregon, where she devotes the majority of her time to pursuing her second love, writing.

Alice loves to hear from readers. You can write her at P.O. Box 755, Brownsville, OR 97327. SASE for reply is appreciated.

Books by Alice Sharpe

HARLEQUIN INTRIGUE

746—FOR THE SAKE OF THEIR BABY
823—UNDERCOVER BABIES
923—MY SISTER, MYSELF*
929—DUPLICATE DAUGHTER*
1022—ROYAL HEIR
1051—AVENGING ANGEL
1076—THE LAWMAN'S SECRET SON**
1082—BODYGUARD FATHER**
1124—MULTIPLES MYSTERY
1165—AGENT DADDY
1190—A BABY BETWEEN THEM
1209—THE BABY'S BODYGUARD

*Dead Ringer
**Skye Brother Babies

CAST OF CHARACTERS

Jack Starling—A year ago this sexy bodyguard was captured during an ambush in Tierra Montañosa. He's returned with one goal: find the woman with whom he spent his last night of freedom and hold her responsible.

Hannah Marks—For months Hannah has felt a stranger's gaze following her every move. The question becomes critical as watching escalates to violence.

Mimi—When Hannah's grandmother is unable to convince Hannah to let her hire Jack to protect her, she goes one better: she hires Jack to protect Hannah's baby.

Aubrielle Marks—Three months old, father unknown (or is he?), adorable and in danger.

Santi Correa—The founder of the Staar Foundation, a man with a lifetime of good work behind him.

David Lengell—Hannah's former boyfriend has been dead for more than a year. Just how involved was this man in what's happening to Hannah now?

Mitch Reynolds—The man who accidentally killed David Lengell.

Hugo Correa—Santi's son, now head of the foundation, was also a hostage. Just how willing—or unwilling—a victim was he? And is he hell-bent on destroying Hannah?

Fran Baker—The Staar Foundation busybody who seems to know it all. Is she in danger or the cause of the rumors and threats against Hannah and her family?

Harrison Plumber—Another surviving hostage of the gunfight and abductions in South America that started it all.

Chapter One

Someone was watching her.

Hannah turned quickly. The three women and one old man behind her in line at the small market either smiled or looked bored. No shifting feet, no averted glances.

"Miss Marks?" the young clerk said, jerking Hannah's attention back to him. He nodded at the debit card in her hand. The groceries were neatly tucked into cloth sacks, ready to go.

"Oh, sorry, Dennis." She ran the card quickly through the machine, determined to get herself under control. But the sensation persisted all across the parking lot and more than once, she stopped to look around, each time expecting to spot someone studying her. Why had she parked at the back of the lot? Finally she was close enough to push the button on her key chain and pop the trunk.

The flat tire taking up two-thirds of the space reminded her she needed to swing by the service station and get it fixed. She'd thought working part-time would be a piece of cake, but there were always errands to run, as well. She fit the bags around the tire and slammed the trunk. That left her looking across the top of the car toward one of Allota's two accessible beaches, this one a narrow span of gray sand leading to the deep blue Pacific Ocean.

It was a cold sea this far north of San Francisco, barely fifty degrees even in summer. On a late May day, with the sun barely peeking from behind high clouds and the wind blowing, just a few hardy souls braved the elements.

A car door slammed nearby and Hannah jumped. She knew she wasn't the only woman in the community to be nervous—there were two unsolved murders of lone women sitting in their cars, both of them parked in their own garages. But she wasn't a lone woman and she didn't park in a garage so there went that excuse.

"Nerves and lack of sleep," her friend and coworker had pronounced when Hannah mentioned the sensation at work. No doubt Fran was right.

Still, it was with a sense of relief that Hannah slipped into the car. What had she done with the keys? Patting pockets proved fruitless. She finally found them stuck in a side pocket of her handbag.

As she bent forward to put the key in the ignition, the passenger door abruptly opened and a man got in beside her. She gasped as impressions struck like stray bullets. Tan skin, long black hair, angular face, straight eyebrows hovering over brilliant blue eyes.

Eyes filled with scathing anger.

She instantly reached for the door handle with one hand and slammed the other down on the horn. He grabbed her hand from the steering wheel and shouted, "Hannah. *¡Parada!*" in the ensuing silence.

With her name and the sound of his voice came recognition. Her hand went limp in his grasp and he released it. Barely able to keep from rubbing her eyes, she whispered, "Jack?"

His eyelids flickered.

"It can't be you," she mumbled.

His shoulders lifted in an elegant shrug and she realized why she hadn't immediately recognized him. He was so much thinner than the last time she'd seen him, so much more weathered. There were a few scars that hadn't been there before, too, one by his nose, another along his jaw. His hair, which had been military short, was now shoulder length, wavy and wild.

Her impulse was to reach for him. "Jack! I thought you were dead—"

He caught her arms in strong hands, stopping her momentum. She fell back in her own bucket seat and after swallowing her shock, murmured, "What's going on?"

"That's what you're going to tell me," he said.

"I don't know what you mean." But of course Aubrielle popped into her mind. Did he know about her? Was that why he was here?

"I want to know who put you up to it, Hannah. Simple as that. Give me a name and I'm out of here."

He'd lost her.

There was a rap on Hannah's window. She looked around to find a very old man with bushy eyebrows peering in at her. She flicked the key to the right and used the switch to power down the window a few inches.

"Everything okay, miss?" he asked, a white handlebar mustache obscuring his lips.

"Everything is fine," she said. She wasn't sure what was going on with Jack, but surely it didn't require outside assistance. "I accidentally hit the horn."

"You positive?" he persisted, his gaze sliding past Hannah to look more closely at Jack. She doubted he was reassured by what he saw.

With more conviction than she felt, she said, "Yes. Thanks."

"If you say so," the old guy said and, leaning his weight on an old wooden cane, shuffled off toward a green sedan, his long raincoat almost dragging on the pavement. Hannah turned back to Jack. "Should I have asked him to call the cops?"

"I'll call the cops myself just as soon as I find out who helped you."

"*You'll* call the cops? Why would you call the cops?"

"I've had months to think," he said with deadly calm. "Months to realize I was conned and you did the conning. Oh, I know you didn't actually kill anyone yourself, but the blood of innocent men is on your hands and you know it."

The relief of realizing his demeanor had nothing to do with Aubrielle quickly gave way to shock as she realized what he was insinuating. "You have to be talking about the ambush down in Tierra Montañosa," she said, stunned he would think— "Are you saying I had something to do with it?"

"That's what I'm saying," he growled.

She took the keys out of the ignition and without consciously deciding to do so, looped a few fingers through the door handle. "I heard you were dead, killed with several other men, buried in a mass grave. How did you get here?"

"I escaped. They butchered the others. As for identifying me—they threw my watch in with the corpses and set the whole thing on fire." He looked away as though catching his breath. Her own seemed to come in short gasps as her imagination provided images of what he'd just described.

"I'm so sorry," she murmured.

His nod was barely perceptible.

She didn't know him well, had only spent one night of her life with him, but he'd helped her that night more than he'd ever, ever know, and now she sincerely wanted to return the kindness. He looked as though he needed it.

On the other hand, it was clear he didn't want anything from her but confirmation of some terrible, ill-conceived suspicion.

"Let me tell you what the Tierra Montañosa government told the Staar Foundation," she said. "The rebel group who carried out the attack call themselves the *Guerrilleros de Tierra Montañosa* although they deny they had anything to do with it. I guess they always do that. Their rhetoric is freedom from tyranny, but the truth is they're a Marxist group. I've read about them since, well, since the ambush. They're terrible people. They—"

He waved away her dialogue. "You think I don't know who they are? I was down there to protect people like you from groups like the GTM. It was my job as a body-guard to know all the organizations and their goals, so don't try to tell me about them. What I want to know is who gave them the inside information to carry out the ambush at Costa del Rio. They had to have inside help to pull that off. They knew where we were going to be and when we were going to be there. You're the one who made the arrangements."

"Yes, I am."

"So who else knew what they were?"

"Until a few minutes before the convoy left, no one knew but you. There'd been threats, we'd been warned to keep it secret."

"What about the founder's son, what's his name, Hugo Correa?"

"What about him?"

"Did he know?"

"No, of course not. You're not suggesting Hugo Correa had anything to do with the rebels, are you?"

"What's wrong? Is it politically incorrect to point a finger at a dead man?"

"Mr. Correa isn't dead."

Jack's brow furrowed. "Run that by me again."

"You don't know?"

"No, damn it. I've been back in the States two weeks. My first thought was to enlist the aid of my sister. I found she was in the middle of her own drama and needed my help. When that was over, I discovered she's pregnant so I left her out of it. As far as Hugo Correa goes, the last I saw of him, he and a couple of the others were being driven away in a truck with about three dozen guerillas pointing assault rifles at their heads. Later we heard they were killed."

"The foundation had kidnap insurance for its officers so they paid off a huge sum to the rebels to get their people back. We heard the rest of you were going to be used to negotiate the release of jailed GTM members."

"It didn't work out that way," he said softly.

"Mr. Correa and the other man were in the hospital for weeks. Apparently Hugo Correa tried to escape by jumping out of the truck and took a bullet in his leg and it got infected. The other man, a guy by the name of Harrison Plumber, had a digestive disease of some kind. As soon as Hugo got out of the hospital, Santi Correa turned over the day-by-day operations of the foundation to his son and more or less resigned."

Jack rubbed his eyes. *"Ah mi dios,"* he mumbled. Looking at her again, he added, "Just tell me who it was."

"Who what was?"

"Who were you working with? And why? Did you do it for money? What other reason could there be, what else could you possibly want from these people?"

"Of course I didn't do it for money!" she said, but the word *money* thundered in her head. *Money.* "I didn't do it all," she mumbled.

"People do terrible things when money is dangled in front of their noses," he said.

She looked out the window at the ocean across the street. *It couldn't be…*

"Hannah?"

She looked at him without really seeing him. She was remembering the day David showed up at her place with a bundle of money he wanted her to keep and had sworn her to secrecy. It had surprised her—their relationship had been a little rocky—and suddenly he was talking about marrying and moving far away.…

How could that have anything to do with this? Yet now that she'd made the connection why couldn't she get it out of her head? She sucked in a tiny breath.

"I know you seduced me the night before the ambush," Jack said. "All I want from you now is the name of the man or woman who put you up to it."

She barely heard him. She had to think. Operating on autopilot, she got out of the car and grabbed her handbag. Her instinct was to walk, to move, to get away.

He was at her side in a moment, taking her arm. One giant question raged like a wildfire through her brain. Had David been involved? And if he had, what did she do now? What *could* she do now?

They crossed the two-lane road to the far side, then threaded their way through rocks, driftwood and seaweed. Jack released her arm and she stumbled up against an old, dead tree lying on its side.

She turned immediately to face Jack. He looked amazing standing in the wind and sun, his white shirt stark against his skin, his cerulean eyes burning. Those eyes now seemed to watch the way she massaged her arm. Did she sense regret at the roughness of his grip? Probably not.

"You've been watching me for days, for weeks," she said, relieved to have finally identified the cause of her uneasiness. Not that it helped much. His being on the scene might explain that creepy someone-is-watching-me feeling, but it was more than compensated for by his accusations and the potential for disaster his presence in Allota could mean. She added, "I've felt your eyes on me."

"No," he said. "I just got to California last night."

"I don't believe you."

"I'm not the one who lies," he said.

She sank down on the log, trying to organize her thoughts. She had to get home—alone. To do that, she had to convince Jack she had nothing to do with the ambush so he would go look under another rock.

Squinting, she peered up at him through strands of windblown hair. "Whether you believe it or not, I'm no more or less than you thought I was the night we met."

"A woman grieving over her boyfriend's death."

Over the guilt. She'd been about to tell David she didn't love him, she wanted him to take his money and go away and then he'd died in a stupid accident. "Mr. Correa told me I could bow out of going with him to

South America for the opening of the new school and I almost did. Everyone blamed my sadness on my grandfather's illness and that was part of it, but the other part was all my inconsistent feelings about David's death. In the end I went and that's where I met you. You'd known David, you were sympathetic and kind. You talked to me, you helped me. It's as simple as that."

"Say it like it is," he insisted, stepping in front of her. Leaning over, he pinned her in place with his arms, his brown hands stark against the bleached wood. He lowered his voice; his face was just inches from hers. "Don't wrap it up in pretty words, *cariño*. Your boyfriend was dead less than a month. We had a couple of drinks, you cried, and then we had raw, messy sex. The next day, I slept in. I never sleep in. I was late leaving you. I felt groggy and slow. I was late getting to the Correa vehicle, too, and I played catch-up until the minute the lead car came across the overturned truck in the middle of the road and all hell broke loose. You weren't there. Why not?"

His single-mindedness beat his words into her head like jungle drums. If this kept up she'd spill her guts, voice her concerns about David to get Jack's focus off her. It was way too soon to do that; there were other people to consider. Struggling to stay calm, she said, "I was already at the school. I left right from the hotel. I wasn't part of the caravan. I had to be there earlier to arrange things on that end."

He shook his head. "So, you had nothing to do with anything."

"No more than you did," she said, and again thought of David and the last time she'd seen him. Oh, no, she had to be wrong. Softening her voice, she added, "If you had been in the car with Hugo Correa, it wouldn't have changed a thing."

"The two men who were in that car died," he said. "They were my men, I should have been there."

"I saw the pictures taken after the incident. I saw what they did. There's no way you would have survived, Jack. It's a miracle anyone did."

"My job was to make sure everyone survived."

"I don't understand you," she said, her voice raspy. "This is no one's fault but the rebels who try to get their way by destroying innocent lives. You know their methods, you know better than anyone what they're capable of. They recruit children. They support drug cartels to finance their so-called patriotism. They murder anyone who wants out. I work for a nonprofit organization started by a man who wanted to improve the education of children in South America, who wanted to help them build a future. How could you think I'd have anything to do with people like the GTM?"

He pushed himself away from her, hitching his hands on his waist as he continued to stare at her face, reaching who knew what conclusions. His gaze was still intense but dare she hope she detected a glimmer of doubt?

A year before, she'd noticed him the minute he walked into the hotel bar to meet with her to go over the plans for the next day. Tall, dark and handsome as the saying goes, and with those blue eyes that could peel the clothes right off a woman. Their attraction had been immediate and mutual, and he was right, the sex had been world-class.

Now, thinner but somehow stronger, less refined and honed by months of deprivation, he still exuded enough sex appeal to topple a dozen women in a single glance. The look in his eyes might not be soft and warm, but it had her sizzling inside and out and she wasn't proud of it.

"I'm leaving," she announced. "I was supposed to be home a half hour ago. Goodbye." She got to her feet and walked a few feet, then turned back to him. "Jack? You believe me, don't you?"

"I don't know," he said.

"I don't know why that bothers me, but it does," she admitted.

He ran a hand through his long hair, clearing his forehead for a moment. "Everything added up," he said as though to himself. "I was so sure it was you."

"I really would like to know how you escaped, Jack. I don't understand why I didn't hear about it on the news."

"Hardly anyone knows I'm back."

"Didn't you go to the consulate? Didn't you need to get a new passport?"

"Not the way I came back into the country."

"Why would you come back illegally? You're a hero—"

"I came back under my own terms to find the truth," he said, looking out to the ocean. "I didn't want to get lost in red tape and protocol. I'll do that later. I have this feeling there's a ticking bomb I can't find."

"Oh, Jack, I'm sorry."

He flashed her a quick glance. "I thought you would have the answers. Now, I'm not so sure."

"I guess I'll have to settle for that," she said. She started to turn again.

"Meet me later tonight," he said suddenly, reaching for her arm, catching her sleeve.

"I can't," she mumbled. "It's impossible."

His fingers slid down her arm, lingered on her hand.

"Come to Fort Bragg for an hour," he said, his voice softer now.

Fort Bragg was several miles south of Allota and was the home of the Staar Foundation. She'd just come from there an hour before. She said, "I'm sorry—"

"Please," he added. "I need to know more about your plans in Costa del Rio. Anything you can remember might help. I have to figure out what's going on down there, Hannah. It's more important than I can tell you. It's bigger than the ambush and a half-dozen deaths. This isn't just about revenge."

Glancing down at their linked fingers, she recalled how bereft she'd been when he disappeared the day after their night together. Coming on the heels of David's death, she'd decided she was a jinx of the worst kind.

After their one wild night together had she anticipated their relationship might continue? The truth? Yes. There was something about Jack Starling—there had been then, there was now. But things had changed and now there was too much at stake to get involved. "I'm sorry," she said, withdrawing her hand. "It's impossible."

"I'm sorry, too," he murmured.

Together, they walked back up the dune. The parking lot had cleared out while she was gone and now Hannah's car was the only one at the back. She'd been away from it less than thirty minutes. The perishables should be okay. Well, maybe not the ice cream…

The explosion wasn't the kind that shook the earth, but was so unexpected, it sent Hannah toppling back against Jack. He immediately swiveled her around as if to shield her from danger, the bodyguard in him coming to the forefront, his strong, warm body pressed against hers.

She looked over his shoulder at the black cloud of smoke enveloping her car.

Chapter Two

At police request, Jack presented his identity, holding his breath it would pass scrutiny. The last name on it was Carlin instead of Starling. It had stood up earlier in the month when he used it, and he assumed it would hold up again. The cops made notes and handed the false driver's license back and then proceeded to ignore him.

Hannah had walked away from him to make a call, and now she tucked her cell phone into her handbag as she returned. She'd seemed desperate to make this call after the explosion. He didn't know if it was because she thought she knew who was behind the bomb or because she was concerned a loved one would hear the news and start to worry.

There was so much he didn't know about her.

Twenty feet farther along, firemen and police were finishing their investigation. The afternoon was giving way to evening, the breeze of earlier in the day getting serious enough to thrash Hannah's straight, shoulder-length hair around her neck. She turned her face into the wind to clear a few glistening strands of red-gold from her mouth and eyes.

She struck him as more contained, less vulnerable and stronger than the last time they'd met. Just as attractive, yes. Just as interesting with a spark of naughty in her clear green eyes. He liked the way her nose tilted up a little at the end, he liked the few freckles scattered across her cheeks.

After seeing and talking to her again it was hard to believe she'd been in on something as nasty as what happened in Tierra Montañosa. He had the gut feeling she was telling the truth, but he had just as strong a feeling she was hiding something he needed to know.

"What did you mean when you accused me of watching you?" Jack asked.

"It's not important," she said, and then looked over his shoulder as something else caught her attention. He turned to find that one of the police officers had detached himself from the others and was walking toward them. With a hasty glance back at Jack, Hannah quickly moved to meet the officer and lowered her head as they spoke. Jack recognized her attempts to keep her conversations private. He'd operated the same way for most of his life.

He swallowed his impatience with her and closed his eyes, searching for the Zen-like spot inside himself he'd learned to access during his months of captivity. For an admitted control freak, there was nothing more humbling than being at the total mercy of merciless men. He'd found the only way to survive with his brain still working was to adapt.

He relaxed tense muscles in his neck and shoulders as the cool ocean breeze blew in his hair and whipped his shirt around his torso. He concentrated on the caw of gulls, the distant sound of waves. The crowd noise receded. He was standing alone, an invisible shaft of energy running through his skull and out the soles of his feet, connecting him to the center of the earth. He was free.

No wire cages. No chains around his neck. No starvation, no guns jabbed into his gut for no reason. No yelling, no threats, no terror.

Part of him yearned to accept that it had all happened the way Hannah said, to get on his bike and go find the rest of his life and never look back. But it wasn't a big part and he knew in his heart it would never happen. He was who he was today because of what had happened to him yesterday. That's the way it worked.

He opened his eyes to find Hannah staring at him. She wore a salmon-colored sweater that somehow matched her lips though he hadn't noticed any lipstick. Until that second he hadn't realized he'd even looked at her lips, but of course he had. If he wanted to torture himself, he could relive the taste of those lips; it wouldn't be the first time. If he wanted to check himself into a mental ward, he could work his memory down each delicious curve and dip of her body.

He'd done that a time or two, as well.

Hannah nodded at something the officer said, and walked toward Jack again, her breasts bouncing gently under her sweater. He suddenly burned with an unexpected need for her.

"I'm getting a ride back to my house, Jack. Officer Latimer asked if you need a lift somewhere."

He glanced toward the other end of the lot and his Harley. Thanks to Ella and Simon, he had it back. "No, thanks."

"Okay. Well, I just want to say goodbye. I'm so glad you're okay. Take care of yourself and try to let the past go. You deserve to be happy now." She put her hands on his shoulders and stood on tiptoe to plant a brief kiss on his left cheek. Her cloud of hair smelled like fresh air.

He caught her hands before she could fly away.

"Why won't you tell me what you meant about being watched?"

"Because it was just my imagination," she said as he reluctantly released her.

"Did you tell the police about it?"

"Yes," she said, but she looked down as she said it, her hand rising to brush at her cheek. He didn't believe her. Why wouldn't she tell the police something like that?

"Someone blew up your car, *cariño*," he said softly. "Maybe you should take it seriously."

"The police assure me the bomb wasn't meant to hurt me. There's been a rash of these things around town," she added, meeting his gaze once again. "They think it was a small bomb on a timer attached to the muffler. Even if I'd been driving the car, I wouldn't have been hurt. The car will need to go to the shop, but they can probably make it good as new. End of story."

"Not the end."

Her hand landed on his arm and she squeezed gently. "Yes. The end. I'm sorry for what you've been through, but maybe it's best this way. Good luck finding what you're looking for. I have to go. Officer Latimer is waving. Goodbye, Jack."

"Wait," he said, but she cast him an apologetic smile before walking briskly to the police car. He watched the vehicle leave the parking lot.

He stood there a moment as the tow truck and the fire truck left, as the few remaining bystanders wandered back to their own lives. Three things occurred to him. One: Hannah was afraid. He knew what fear looked like, what it smelled like, how it sounded. He didn't think she was afraid of him. So, what was she frightened of?

Two: She did not want him to know where she lived. Why?

Three: She seemed to think that by not inviting him, he would stay away.

THE HOUSE SHE NOW SHARED with her grandmother was less than a mile from the ocean, tucked into a small neighborhood on a wooded street. As always, coming home calmed something deep in Hannah's soul. Especially tonight when she felt as though she'd dodged a bullet named Jack.

Hannah's grandmother, Mimi Marks, was a comfortable woman of seventy-three who wore her long gray hair in braids, was partial to denim overalls and big plastic clog-like shoes in bright colors. Back in the day, she'd helped her husband build this little house. On Friday nights, it was a sure thing she and a small pack of other women could be found drinking beer and playing poker at one or another of their homes.

She met Hannah at the door and held her at arm's length. She was wearing a knee-length Astroturf-green cardigan with orange and brown stripes near the hem. She was as earthy as Hannah's recently remarried mother was snooty and a million times easier to get along with. In fact, Hannah's grandparents had more or less raised Hannah.

"Tell me the truth," Mimi insisted. "Are you really okay?"

"I really am. Like I told you on the phone, I wasn't even in the car."

"Who would pull a stunt like that?" Without waiting for an answer, she added, "I've had a dozen calls from people all over Allota. They say the police claim it's a pack of rowdy Fort Bragg kids."

The Allota grapevine was alive and well. "I gather it's happened before. Is Aubrielle all right?"

"Of course she is. I fed her the milk you expressed." Mimi smiled and patted Hannah's arm. "Go on, look at her, I know it's killing you. Dinner will be potluck seeing as we don't have anything from the store."

"We'll take your car shopping tomorrow," Hannah said as she quickly walked down the short hall, past Mimi's room but not as far as her own bedroom and office, pausing at the door to the nursery.

Painted pink the day the results of the ultrasound revealed the baby was a girl, the small room was frilly and fluttery and probably silly, but it never ceased to make Hannah smile. Her grandmother, who had wanted to paint it lime-green and canary-yellow, just shook her head.

But it was the three-month-old baby in the crib that drew Hannah. She crossed the floor without bothering to make her steps quiet, hoping the baby would wake up, needing to see her, touch her, and heaven knows, nurse her.

Aubrielle's eyes were open. Hannah lifted the baby to her shoulder, where the infant made some very sweet sounds and Hannah's heart felt as though it was going to burst.

She glanced at the nursery door to make sure it was closed, and then she took a deep breath. Whispering into the warm little ear by her lips, she said, "I saw your daddy today."

There, she'd said it out loud for the first time. Jack Starling was Aubrielle's father. One night of sex had created the most wonderful gift in the world.

"I want you to know I will not allow him to mess things up for you, sweetheart, I promise that," Hannah continued. "It's you and me, we're a family. I'm not going to risk a near stranger demanding half your destiny so don't worry, it's okay. It's our secret."

They moved to the rocking chair where Hannah nursed her baby, tears burning behind her nose. She hated lying, she knew she was bad at it, she even knew Jack deserved the truth, but she could not, would not, risk Aubrielle's safety. Jack was a bodyguard, a man's man, and what little Hannah knew of his life had nothing to do with being a father. Take his current obsession. With little to go on but a hunch, he was running around accusing innocent people of terrible crimes. He'd entered the country without a passport. Maybe being stuck in the jungle for almost a year had fried his brain.

She was avoiding thinking about David and Tierra Montañosa and the ambush at Costa del Rio, she knew that. For a second it occurred to her that David couldn't have been involved—he'd died weeks before the trip—and a mountain of worry lifted from her shoulders. He hadn't even been to Costa del Rio; he was the foundation pilot in the States. How could he be involved?

Where had the money come from weeks before the ambush? Why had he told her to keep it a secret?

And just like that she thought of the original gym bag David had left with her. Where was it? In her home office? No. She'd taken it to work, she remembered that. Then she'd transferred the cash into her briefcase. Was there another paper in the bag? She seemed to remember there was though she also recalled dismissing it. What had she done with the gym bag? Where was it? Had it gone with her to the locker or was it still in the bottom of the file cabinet in the locked drawer?

It was no use, she couldn't remember, but that was easily fixed; she could look.

Closing her eyes, she found Jack's image front and center, not David's. Jack's eyes. His mouth. When he called her *cariño,* her insides melted. She remembered their one night in vivid detail, images burned on her brain and enhanced by all that came afterward.

As she rested her head against the wooden spindles of the chair, Hannah's gaze drifted out the window to the slice of dark sky visible between the even darker branches. She'd positioned the chair just this way so that would be her view, but suddenly it seemed more oppressive than comforting. She couldn't fight the feeling someone was looking in at them. The lights in the room seemed garish; she felt as though she was on a stage.

This was melodramatic, but the feeling wouldn't go away. Who could possibly be out there? Maybe Jack was right, maybe she should have told the police about her feelings, but the thought of going through an investigation while Jack was around frightened her. She wanted him to leave California. If she was still spooked after he was gone, she'd talk to Officer Latimer. He'd seemed approachable.

Aubrielle soon fell back asleep. Superaware of the window, Hannah adjusted her own clothing before carefully lifting the drowsy baby. She nuzzled Aubrielle's soft, sweet skin before putting her back in her crib, then made sure the window was locked, the curtains closed tight. She turned off the light as she left the room and looked back. The little pink mushroom-shaped nightlight illuminated very little but gave the cozy space a rosy hue. Aubrielle was safe. That's all that mattered.

While walking down the hall, Hannah heard a man's deep voice and thought it was the television until her grandmother's bright chirp responded. Still spooked from the events of the afternoon, she hurried into the living room. What now?

Her grandmother sat on the red plaid sofa. Jack Starling sat in the bright blue chair set at a right angle, a wineglass cradled in his hands. They both looked up as Hannah made an abrupt halt.

Jack put down his glass and stood. With his unruly black hair and stormy expression he looked like a slightly disreputable action hero plopped down in the middle of Snow White's cottage.

Mimi popped off the couch. "Your friend has been telling me stories about your trip to Tierra Montañosa last year. Well, you know, honey, you never talk about it. Anyway, I've convinced him to stay for dinner, though heaven knows what we're going to give him to eat. Hannah, you look bushed. Sit down, dear, I'll get you a glass of wine." She scurried toward the kitchen on her mission.

"How did you find out where I live?" Hannah demanded in a low voice.

"I told the clerk inside the store that you forgot something. He told me. Apparently his wife's mother plays cards with your grandmother. That's the nice thing about a small town."

"But why did you come? What do you want now?"

He sat back down in his chair. "I'm just making sure you're okay."

"No, you're not."

"No, I'm not," he agreed. "I'm here because you're hiding something." He pulled on her hand and she perched on the corner of the sofa, her knees almost touching his. "Why are you so nervous?" he asked.

"Why are you staying for dinner?"

"Your grandmother invited me."

Mimi reappeared with wine for Hannah. Smiling broadly, the older woman hitched her hands on her waist. "Now, you two catch up on old times while I figure out what we're going to eat." She took a few steps, then turned back. "Oh, Jack, did you know a Frenchman down in Costa del Rio?"

"French?"

"Yes. I'm sure he was very dashing. An expatriate."

"No, I'm sorry. I don't recall anyone from France."

"I thought maybe you knew him. I mean, you lived down there for a couple of years, right? Hannah was only down there a few days and you said you spent one evening with her and then—"

"Grandma, what about dinner?" Hannah said softly, doing her best to avert a disaster.

In a scolding voice, Mimi said, "I just thought it would be nice to hear about the baby's father from someone else. You won't tell me much about him."

Hannah must have made a strangled sound in her throat because both her grandmother and Jack glanced at her. "I know we're not supposed to talk about him," Mimi said with a defiant tilt to her chin. "I know you said he was a giant mistake, but I just thought—"

"Jack didn't know him," Hannah said, praying for some kind of diversion. It was the West Coast, for heaven's sake. Where was a 6.0 earthquake when you needed one?

"I didn't know you had a baby," Jack said.

Mimi, looking perplexed, muttered, "I told you Hannah was in with Aubrielle when you got here."

"I assumed Aubrielle was another adult."

Mimi's defiance was melting into contrition. "I'll go see to dinner," she said.

As soon as she was out of the room Jack cleared his throat. "*You* have a baby."

Hannah took a gulp of wine and sighed. "Yes."

"How old?"

"Three months."

"Three months. Funny, I don't recall a French expatriate." His eyebrows raised up his forehead, his eyes narrowed. "Three months. Oh, God, Hannah—is this my...my baby?"

He looked horrified at the thought. *Good.* She said, "Aubrielle is *not* your baby."

"But the timing—"

"No."

"Is she David's?"

After a moment, Hannah nodded.

"Why wouldn't you tell your grandmother that your baby is your boyfriend's child?"

"It's complicated."

"Try me."

"There were rules at the foundation about dating and David and I broke them. David is gone now, there's nothing to be gained by bringing all this up. I might even lose my job and I need it."

"It sounds like a lot of justifying," Jack said.

"Of course it is. That's what happens when you mess things up. You do your best to make them better." She took a deep breath, smoothed her jeans over her thighs and added, "My grandmother didn't know David well and certainly never knew anything about us being a couple. As you can see, she's not much for secrets. And then there was David's family to consider. His parents have about twelve other grandchildren and live thousands of miles away. They know nothing about me. I just decided to tell a select few people Aubrielle's father was a man I met when I was in South America who is totally out of our lives,"

"Then you were pregnant when we met?"

She looked him in the eye and nodded.

"If she's three months old, it must have happened—"

"The last night David was alive, yes."

"Correct me if I'm wrong, but wasn't part of the reason you were grieving so much that you felt bad you'd been about to break up with him?"

"You never had sex with someone you weren't sure about?" she countered.

"Point taken. He died the next morning on his way to work, right?"

"He was riding his bike. The truck driver said David hit a patch of loose gravel and fell right into the road."

Jack stared at her for a few dozen jumpy heartbeats and then nodded. "You know, I've decided to believe your claim that you had nothing to do with what happened down in Costa del Rio."

She blinked at the change of subject before saying, "Good. Why?"

"I'm not sure. You're smart enough and clever enough and maybe even sneaky enough, but you're not ruthless."

"That's true. I'm relieved to hear you say it."

"But you do know or suspect something. Who are you protecting?"

She drained the wine from the stemmed glass and set it down. It was time to put this matter to rest. Her voice a little on the stern side, she leaned toward him. "Let's get this straight. You're a stranger I spent one amazing night with a year ago. Like you so graphically pointed out this afternoon, it was sex and nothing more.

I'm not going to offer excuses, but seeing you again is embarrassing—it wasn't exactly my most shining hour. Is that blunt enough for you?"

"It's excellent. If I was capable of being shamed, that would have done it." He paused a second and added, "An 'amazing' night, huh?" the skin crinkling around his eyes as he smiled.

She glared at him.

Mimi yelled from the kitchen, "We're having stir-fried tofu and veggies."

"My grandmother thinks she can cook," Hannah said softly. "She can't."

Jack shrugged. "I never turn down a meal."

When she didn't smile, he added, "I'd like to see David's kid and I really am hungry."

She stood up. He was a danger to her, to her baby, to the future. He needed to go away so she could figure out what if anything to do with her ever-growing suspicions. Maybe in the end he'd be the one to share them with, but not now. What would happen if she convinced him to leave for a week or so with the promise she would poke around a little when she went into the office? Maybe Fran knew something. As the head of HR, she seemed to know something about everyone.

"You're suddenly a light-year away," Jack said, coming to stand in front of her.

She pushed her hair back from her forehead. "It's been a terrible day, Jack. I feel like I'm being stalked by the invisible man and now you're accusing me of helping a killer. Give me a number where I can call you should something come to mind. For now, I'm going to go wash up for dinner and when I get back, I would really like to find you made your apologies to my grandmother and left. Is that too much to ask?"

"Yeah, it is," he said. "I already lost a few days with my family. Time is passing."

"The ambush happened almost a year ago. Another week or two won't matter."

"It's not that simple," he said. "I told you this isn't just about revenge."

She stared at him and he stared at her. They were at an impasse. This was crazy, this was her house, well, her grandmother's house. What made Jack Starling think he could just refuse to leave?

When his gaze strayed past her face to the plate-glass window behind her back, she wondered if he was looking at their reflections. In the next instant, he lunged at her. She gasped at the unexpectedness of it. He wrapped his arms around her and spun her around to the floor where she landed on her back with a crash. He flung his body on top of hers, using his arms to surround her head. She pushed on his solid chest but he held tighter.

A loud popping sound was followed by a distant scream and other unidentifiable sounds that rumbled in Hannah's brain. Ragged cubes of glass rained down on them like pebbles, bouncing on the furniture, skittering across the hardwood floors.

Jack held her even tighter. She swallowed a scream as her thoughts went to Aubrielle.

Chapter Three

"What in the hell is going on?" Jack demanded. He'd pulled Hannah to her feet, safety glass tumbling from both their clothes.

"I don't know," Hannah said, eyes wide with fear.

"Like hell you don't."

Mimi entered from the kitchen. "Look at the window!" she cried and Jack and Hannah both turned to look at the gaping hole where the window had been. "Did someone shoot it out?"

"I think it was a brick," Jack said.

Hannah was trying to shake the glass off her clothes as she moved toward the hallway. He heard the cries of a very small baby coming from farther back in the house.

Mimi intercepted her granddaughter. "You'll get glass all over her. I'll go." She hurried off down the hall and Hannah turned to face him.

"Hannah?" he said. "What's going on?"

It looked as though she wanted to tell him to mind his own business, but this time the flippancy with which she'd treated the car bomb was gone. In fact, the fear in her eyes yanked at him.

"I don't have the slightest idea."

"But it's something that's been going on for a while, isn't it?"

"No," she said, and looked surprised by the idea. And then a knowing look crept into her eyes. "Maybe," she admitted. "I'm not sure. Nothing like this, though. Well, the break-in, but nothing of consequence was taken. Did you see someone outside before this happened?"

"I saw a car slow down outside and then speed up. What break-in?"

"You have remarkable reflexes," she said, still dusting glass off her clothes.

"What break-in?"

"It happened before I moved in with Grandma. Someone broke into my old apartment. The police investigated, nothing was taken, that was all there was to it."

He frowned, trying to make sense of the break-in, the bomb and the broken window and coming up empty. Was it possible the events were related to Tierra Montañosa? Without knowing more about Hannah's life, how could he make that kind of determination?

He looked around the floor until he found a brick-sized rock under a small table. Crunching glass under his feet, he retrieved the rock, using one of the little doilies that were draped over the arms of the sofa. There was a piece of lined paper tied to the rock with an ordinary-looking length of white string.

"Do you have plastic gloves?" he asked.

She had her head upside down and was shaking out the glass. As she swung her head up and back, her sweater rode up her trim midriff, exposing a creamy strip of skin. With her hair tousled and her clothes askew, she looked as though she'd just gotten out of bed, and once again, his body started a slow burn.

"In the kitchen under the sink," she said, pulling down on her sweater. "I have to check on Aubrielle."

With that she disappeared down the hall, the sway of her hips mesmerizing.

"Get a grip," he mumbled as he shook off most of the glass. Leaving the cloth and rock on top of the television, he moved into the kitchen, where the smell of burned vegetables greeted him. The pan had been taken off the heat but the glob inside it looked pretty horrendous. He'd eaten worse, though.

He found the plastic gloves where Hannah said they were.

Hannah and her grandmother were both back in the living room when he returned. "She went right back to sleep," Hannah said, pausing to look up from her task. She'd found a broom and a dustpan and was working on sweeping up the glass. A vacuum cleaner sat off to the side, awaiting its turn.

It took him a second to realize she was talking about her baby. He said, "Oh. Good."

As the cold night blew right into the room through the gaping hole, Jack took time to go outside to Hannah's grandfather's shop where Mimi assured him he'd find a roll of plastic and a staple gun. It was killing him not to investigate the note first, but he guessed with a baby in the house, certain protocols had to be observed.

At last things were secure. Hannah insisted on unwrapping the note herself, announcing she was certain she was the intended recipient. As the plastic gloves were two sizes too small for his hands, he didn't object. He and Mimi crowded around the table where Hannah had settled with the rock.

The paper turned out to be ordinary notebook paper,

words cut from a magazine and glued on. It was the message that was startling.

"The bomb wasn't the work of kids. Stop what you're doing—or else."

Swiveling to look at Hannah, Jack and Mimi both said, "What *are* you doing?"

"Nothing," Hannah said. "Absolutely nothing."

"Are you sure?"

"Yes," she said, her voice reflecting the strain of the past hour.

"First the car, then this," Mimi said.

"This could have hurt someone," Hannah said. "It could have hurt Aubrielle. Why? I haven't done anything to anyone."

"Someone thinks you have," Jack said.

"Who?"

There was no answer to that and the three of them stared at the note a while longer until Jack added, "How did this person know you think the car bomb was the work of kids?"

"Because that's what the police told Hannah in the middle of a public parking lot," Mimi said with a dismissive note in her voice. "Everyone in Allota knows what everyone else knows, more or less." Pushing herself to her feet, she added, "Listen, you two, I'm starving and my lovely stir-fry is now beyond redemption. We'll all think better if we eat something. I'm going into town to pick up some Chinese at Shanghai Lo." She grabbed her keys and handbag off a hook. "Everybody like beef and broccoli? Maybe some wonton soup?"

Jack said, "Fine." Hannah didn't seem to hear her grandmother.

Once the older woman was gone, Hannah rubbed her forehead and began pacing the living room. She finally faced Jack. "I have to take a shower and get the rest of the glass out of my hair before the baby wakes up again. Would you mind listening for her? Then you can be on your way."

He'd rather get into the shower with Hannah. "Sure, I can listen for her."

Forehead creasing, she said, "Don't pick her up, though, just bang on the bathroom door."

"I won't touch her," he said with a dry edge to his voice.

When he heard the water running, he did his best not to let his imagination run away with him. He'd taken one shower with Hannah, one very long, languid shower in the middle of a tropical night. He'd lifted her against the aqua tile and she'd wrapped her legs around him. Water had drummed on their heads; he could still see beads of it rolling down her throat and across her breasts. The heat burning between them had rivaled the one hundred percent humidity outside. That particular memory had been his constant companion the first few weeks of captivity.

He heard little mewling sounds and took a deep breath, letting useless memories float away. Time to go see if David's kid was awake or if he was hearing things.

The only room with a light on turned out to be the pinkest place he'd ever seen. He was almost afraid to enter, but he heard the sound again. Switching on a lamp, he all but tiptoed across the carpet and looked down into the crib.

The baby was so tiny! He stared at her for several moments, transfixed at her absolute vulnerability. He could even see the blue veins under her skin. Her head was covered with a brown fuzz.

She didn't seem to be actually awake; she was just jerking and making little sounds, screwing her face up and then smiling at nothing, bubbles on her lips. It was the closest he'd ever been to a baby.

David's baby. Damn.

He'd known David in the Marines. David had been a helicopter pilot, he'd been a sniper, and for a while they'd flown a few missions together. Eventually they lost touch but by then, Jack had seen tendencies in David he hadn't much liked. A certain disdain for the truth, a predilection for shortcuts that sometimes ended up costing other men dearly, an every-man-for-himself kind of mentality that included money under the table when the opportunity arose.

In a way, maybe it was better David had died. Jack could no more imagine the David he knew being a decent father than he could imagine it of himself. Then again, as he'd recently learned, if a man lived long enough, he had a chance to redeem himself.

Had David done that? With Hannah, he'd earned the trust of a pretty remarkable woman, so maybe he had.

"Is she awake?" Hannah asked from the doorway.

Startled, he turned with a guilty smile. He'd been about to run a finger along Aubrielle's cheek, curious to know if she was as soft as she looked.

"I think she's waking up," he said, and backed away from the crib as though the baby was a ticking bomb about to detonate. Hannah glided past him on the way to her child, the scent of flowers lingering in her wake. She'd changed into black slacks and a black sweater that offset her porcelain skin. Her reddish hair was wet and unexpectedly wavy. She looked fresh and sexy. He had to remind himself to take a breath.

"I know you must have a lot to do," she said as she

reached into the crib and picked up her daughter. She turned to face him and said, "Thanks for the help tonight."

"Cut it out," he said.

"Jack—"

"We're going to talk. I'm not going anywhere until we do."

She sighed heavily. "I have to nurse the baby. You could wait in the living room—"

"No, you do what you have to do. I'll turn my back if you want, but we're going to talk now." He turned his back and crossed his arms.

After a few seconds of rustling sounds and the creak of rockers, she said, "I'm not going to talk to your back, Jack. Go ahead and turn around."

He did, leaning against the doorjamb. Hannah was modestly draped in a pink blanket. All Jack could see of Aubrielle was one tiny foot and an equally tiny hand. Determined to set things straight, he said, "You need help, Hannah."

"No."

"Whatever is going on is over your head."

"If you mean I don't understand why anyone would want to hurt me, yes, you're right."

"You know what I find kind of puzzling?"

She looked at him as though worried what he'd say next. "What?"

"You didn't call the cops about the window."

"What could they do?"

"Investigate. Take the note and try to trace—"

"White paper and cut-out words? A rock?"

"Ever heard of fingerprints? Tire tracks out on the drive? Neighbors who saw something?"

"Jack, what do you suppose is the first thing the

police would do?" When he shrugged in response, she continued. "They would investigate you. You're new in town. Why are you here, how do you know me, etc. Maybe your false identity would hold up under closer scrutiny, maybe it wouldn't."

"That concerns me, not you," he said.

"Because you're at my house, it concerns me, too, and what concerns me concerns my baby."

"Your grandmother can't file a claim with her home owner's insurance if she doesn't report the attack," he said reasonably.

"She's afraid to make a claim on her insurance because she's afraid they'll cancel her policy. I have an emergency fund. I'll buy her a new window."

He let it drop.

"I'll make you a deal," she added. "If you leave now, I'll call the cops and tell them about the window and how I've felt as though I'm being watched. I'll give them the rock and the paper. We won't have to inform the insurance company if Grandma doesn't want to, but the authorities will be advised. You'll get your way."

He shook his head. "Not until you're honest with me. I want to know who you're protecting. I figure it must be someone at the Staar Foundation."

She narrowed her eyes. "Not that again—"

"I haven't told you what I saw out in the jungle," he said.

The baby started crying. Hannah deftly manipulated baby and blanket against her chest and stood. "Turn around so I can fix my bra," she said.

With an internal smile, he did as she asked. Funny how shy people could be around someone they'd once been so blatantly intimate with.

"Okay," she said, and patting the baby's tiny back, demanded, "What did you see?"

He pushed himself away from the jamb. He wished she'd come closer to him so he could speak in a whisper instead of across a room. The things he had to say weren't the kind of things a man wanted to shout.

As she resettled in the rocker, he looked around the room until he spied a small wooden toy chest. Pulling that close to her chair, he parked himself on top of it, forearms resting on his thighs.

"First of all, the guerillas knew about me. About my training and the fact that I'd been a mercenary for a short time a while ago. They treated me differently than the others, singling me out. At first I thought it was because I spoke the language, but then I realized they were kind of grooming me, seeing if I might turn tail and help them."

Her eyes grew wide. "What did you do?"

"I had nothing to do with them until after they killed the other hostages. Then I considered the possibility that if I ever wanted to escape, I had better seem to be more cooperative. So I turned into a model prisoner and kept my eyes open."

"I don't—"

"I'm going to cut this short. I think the Staar Foundation is the front for the GTM, that they are supporting terrorist schools and camps. I have to find out who is involved and how deeply."

"That's absurd. Santi Correa and his son, Hugo, would never—"

"How do you know? How do you really know that?"

She was silent for several seconds. "Couldn't you just

tell our government or the Tierra Montañosa government about your suspicions and let them investigate?"

"The minute the GTM realized I escaped, you can bet the camps I was shown disappeared, but they're still there, further underground or in a different spot. They were working up to something big. Right before I left, they were practicing some sort of mock invasion or takeover of some kind."

"What do you mean?"

"I mean they practiced entering blocked-off areas that represented buildings and killing and subduing mock representations of people. As for telling our government—governments don't move fast, they launch studies. Just verifying my true identity and being viewed as a credible witness given the way I entered the country would take forever."

"Don't get me wrong," she said, "I can see you're truly concerned about this, but it has nothing to do with what's happening to me—"

"Doesn't it? Are you sure?"

He could see by the look in her eyes that she wasn't sure at all.

He took her free hand in his. "Hannah, even if this is unrelated to you, the fact remains you and your family are in danger. You have to take the threat seriously. You've mentioned small things going wrong, but these things today aren't small, they're meant to terrify you. The bomb could have easily been big enough to destroy your car and everyone near it. The rock through the window could have been a bullet. Since you aren't aware of what you're doing that has someone reacting this way, you can't even stop doing it."

"If I go to the police I'll have to tell them all this," she countered. "They'll check into everyone's lives and if you're wrong, we could irreparably damage the reputation of a wonderful nonprofit organization. I'm not doubting these schools exist, I'm just doubting your conclusion that the Staar Foundation is connected to them. I'm sure the GTM has camps everywhere."

"You haven't been listening to me."

"Yes, I have, Jack," she said, and firmly reclaimed her hand. "I'm just not convinced."

"Then why are you protecting someone?"

"Oh, no, not that again."

He shook his head. "Listen, no matter what you think, I'm here and I'm not going to go away until I get to the bottom of this."

"I guess that's your decision. It doesn't include me. We had one night a long time ago…"

"Then let me be your bodyguard. That way we can pool what we know, we can work together and I can protect you. I need a place to hang out while I snoop around—"

"No way. I don't need protection."

"Really? Do you actually believe that?"

"Of course I believe it. It won't work. You have to leave."

"You're wrong," came a voice from behind Jack's back. He swiveled around to find Mimi standing just inside the room.

"Grandma—" Hannah began.

"You're wrong, Hannah Marie. Ever since your grandpa died and you got pregnant, you've been trying to do everything alone. You need help. *We* need help."

"Maybe we do," Hannah said reluctantly, and then with a swift glance at Jack, added, "But not this man."

Mimi made a big deal of looking around the room and behind her. "Then, which man, Hannah?"

"Grandma—"

"I'll hire you," Mimi said, looking directly at Jack.

"You don't even know Jack Starling," Hannah muttered.

The older woman nodded abruptly. "You're right, I don't. But I like him, and so do you."

Jack smiled.

"I do not *like* him," Hannah grumbled.

"Whatever. Okay, if you won't allow me to hire him as a bodyguard for you, then I'll hire him as one for my great-granddaughter. It'll be good having a man here protecting her. You accept, Mr. Starling?"

"I accept," Jack said quickly before Hannah could get in another word.

Chapter Four

"You can sleep here," Hannah said a few hours later when everything had quieted down again. Aubrielle slept in her crib, which Hannah had pushed into her own bedroom. No way was she leaving her baby alone in a room with a big window. Mimi had long since excused herself to go to bed and Jack, who refused to leave even to drive back to Fort Bragg and check out of his motel, had finally stopped bombarding her with questions.

Standing next to her, he perused the room that had been her grandfather's den until his death. The walls were still lined with shelves of books, but the desk was gone, shoved into Hannah's room where she used it to work from home. In its place was the futon they'd installed for the occasional overnight guest. The closet was stuffed with boxes that were too heavy to cart up to the attic.

The fact was, Hannah realized, it was like there were three of them crowded into the small room: herself, Jack and the memory of their first and only night together. That memory had somehow assumed an identity of its own, a mass larger than the sum of the two of them combined. It vibrated with suspended breath as it hovered and waited.

"*Cariño,*" Jack said, his eyes dark in the deep

shadows, the undercurrents of desire she could taste in the air between them sharp and poignant…and impossible.

"We need to get something out in the open," she said softly.

He moved past her, gently brushing her breasts with his arm. As he had nothing to unpack, he turned upon reaching the futon, sat down, patted the mattress beside him and said, "I'm all ears."

She crossed to the closet, yanked open the door and caught a sleeping bag as it fell from its perch atop a stack of cardboard boxes. She tossed it at him and grabbed a pillow. "A lot has happened since we met," she said, still way too aware of him. When he opened his mouth to respond, she held up a finger. "To both of us, I mean. Nothing is the same. We're not the same. You may have railroaded yourself into my grandmother's house, but you can't—"

"Railroad myself into your bed?" he finished for her.

Holding the pillow against her chest, she nodded.

He tossed the bag down on the futon, stood up and walked back to stand in front of her. "I don't force myself into a woman's bed. I wait to be invited."

The last time they'd met, she'd done the inviting and he knew it. This time she met his gaze and said, "Then we'll be fine because I won't be asking."

He leaned forward and whispered, "That's too bad." Then, his voice serious, he added, "Your grandmother mentioned you go to work twice a week and do the rest of your work from your home office. You don't go in again until the day after tomorrow, right?"

Remembering the promise of the paper she'd found with David's money that might or might not help matters, she said, "Actually, I need to go in tomorrow for a few minutes. Uh, I need to make a copy of a report brought home from work that got destroyed in the car bomb today. Plus we're all working more hours because of a big Founder's Day open house planned for next weekend."

The look he directed her way was suspicious. "I don't think—"

"Let's remember exactly who you've been hired to guard," she warned him. "Don't try to tell me what to do."

He threw up his hands in mock surrender. "I wouldn't dream of it."

"Because your number one priority is keeping my baby safe or didn't you mean what you said about being her bodyguard?"

"Of course I meant it. But the big picture—"

"Yes, I know. But if you're going to stay in my grandmother's house, then you pay your way by thinking of Aubrielle first."

"Sure," he said. "Of course. But that means tomorrow you tell me what you're so determined not to say tonight. We have to work together, Hannah, and we have to start immediately."

It was well after midnight and the day's events had finally battered their way through Hannah's defenses, so she didn't push further.

"Do you have a gun?" she asked.

"No."

"My grandfather had a rifle and a shotgun," she said.

"I know. Your grandmother told me where they are." He dug in his pocket and produced the small gold key that locked the gun cabinet in the living room. "I'm kind of hoping I won't need to use a weapon," he said, flipping the key in the air and catching it. It disappeared back in his pocket.

Hannah refused to think about the fact that Mimi was so spooked she'd handed this man a key to the guns within hours of meeting him. "And if you do need to use one?"

"Then I will." He put his hands on her shoulders and stared down at her. Despite her best intentions, her pulse throbbed in her throat. His mouth mesmerized her as a sensuous smile lifted one corner of his upper lip. She prepared herself for—well, for anything. Why deny the fact she was attracted to him as she'd never been attracted to anyone before? It didn't mean she had to act on it, but pretending it didn't exist wasn't working, either.

"Go to bed," he whispered.

She escaped with her pride barely intact but she slept like a rock, so lost in unidentifiable dreams that the next morning, it was clear Aubrielle had been crying for a while. After taking care of her tiny daughter's needs, she carried her into the living room.

The plastic on the window served as a vivid reminder of the rock and the attached warning that had sailed through the night before. Juggling Aubrielle and the phone book, she found the number of the one and only place in town that handled things like broken windows and arranged for an estimate.

What did the person who threw the rock think she was doing? That was the big question and though she'd racked her brain a million times in the past twelve hours for an explanation, she simply couldn't think of one.

She mothered her baby, she did her work, she

shopped—her life was a little on the predictable side for bombs and rocks and threatening notes.

She found Jack in the kitchen with her grandmother, the two of them reading the paper and eating burned toast like long-lost friends. Jack was wearing the same clothes as the day before—a little more crumbled now as though he'd slept in them. It didn't matter. Clean as a whistle, slightly rumpled—he looked good no matter what his condition. In fact, the beard darkening his jaw-line seemed to make his eyes all the more blue.

Hannah had dressed for work in a black jacket and trim skirt. As soon as Mimi saw her, she got to her feet and laid claim to her great-granddaughter, transferring the baby and blanket in an effortless manner, but Hannah noticed the sideways glance at Jack and the nod of her head.

"What's going on?" Hannah asked as she poured herself a cup of coffee.

"Nothing," Mimi said quickly.

Jack cleared his throat. "Well, actually—"

"My poker ladies are all due in half an hour," Mimi said while rocking Aubrielle in her arms. "It's way too early for pretzels and beer. I'll make tea. Are there cookies in the freezer?"

"I don't know," Hannah said. "Since when does your poker group meet on a Tuesday morning?" Looking from Mimi to Jack, she added, "Okay, you two, what's up?"

"Nothing. Barb and the others are coming over to keep me and Aubrielle company while you and Jack go do your reconnoitering. Did you call the glass people yet, dear?"

Hannah took a sip of coffee brewed twice as strong, no, three times as strong, as her grandmother made it.

Didn't take a genius to figure out who started the coffee maker that morning. "They'll be here at ten o'clock. What do you mean, 'reconnoiter'?"

"I want to see foundation headquarters," Jack said.

"I don't think that's such a great idea," she said.

"Plus, I figure you probably need to take care of some kind of insurance thing with the garage concerning your car and I have to check out of the hotel by 10:00 a.m. We could take my Harley but it's a little on the conspicuous side. Mimi has generously offered us the use of her car."

"And the poker crew?"

"I don't want anyone to be alone in this house until we figure out what's going on. Alone anywhere, for that matter."

"So five ladies over seventy are going to keep my baby safe? I thought you were Aubrielle's bodyguard."

"I think the best way to keep Aubrielle safe is to figure out why someone wants to scare her mother half to death. For this particular morning, this is the plan. It'll give us a chance to talk and begin cementing our new pact. We're a team, remember?"

There was no need to ask what he wanted to talk about. Again she thought of the front window and the rock and what it could portend. What was the point of trying to protect David? Besides, if Jack got to the bottom of this, he'd leave and that was a good thing. "Okay," she said, then, looking at each of them in turn, added, "No more making sneaky plans behind my back."

"Of course, dear," Mimi said. "Don't forget to stop by the store and get something for dinner. I made another list. It's there by the door."

"And you'll call my cell if there's any sign of trouble?"

"Don't you worry about a thing."

Jack pushed himself to his feet. "Mimi, I know you're familiar with the rifle, so we'll take the shotgun. That okay with you?"

"Damn tootin'," she said. "No one will get close to Aubrielle with me and the poker ladies here."

Hannah did her best not to shudder.

CHECKING IN AT THE GARAGE TOOK no time at all and soon they were on their way to Fort Bragg. The road traveled up the hills out of Allota, following the coastline south. Jack drove Mimi's small white car expertly, manipulating it around the hair-raising curves with ease.

"The road reminds me of some of those in Tierra Montañosa," he said.

"Curvy and steep," she said, agreeing.

They stopped at Jack's motel first and she waited in the car while he collected his things and settled the bill. When he walked back across the parking lot, he carried just a leather backpack slung over one broad shoulder and a leather jacket looped through his arm. The wind was blowing again—it just about always blew in the late spring—whipping his long, dark hair around his face. He'd changed into a clean dark shirt and black jeans and as his gaze swept the parking lot for who knew what, she thought he looked dangerous.

He *was* dangerous.

As he got back into the car, she whispered, "How did you escape the GTM?"

"It's not a pretty story," he said, glancing at her and away. "Nothing you want to hear."

"Yes, I do," she said. "Of course I do."

He kind of grunted a response.

"Jack, please. I want to know."

He took a deep breath and stared out the windshield. Just when she'd about given up expecting a response, he started talking, his voice intense. "I realized one night they'd made camp relatively close to civilization." A knot appeared and disappeared in his jaw. "I'd buddied up to one of the guards. He'd grown kind of careless around me, so that night when he came to take away the food bowl, I took advantage of that situation and turned his weapon on him." Again he fell into silence.

Hannah took a deep breath. It was obvious that using the guard's trust to overthrow him had been hard for Jack, that it had struck him as a dishonorable thing to do and that surprised her.

Before she could respond, he slid her a piercing look, daring her to comment. She held her tongue. What did she know of these kinds of decisions?

He finally said, "I killed anyone who tried to stop me. I don't know how many men died, it all happened in a blur." Again he glanced at her as he added, "It was either me or them." His eyes didn't look as though he believed his own words.

"Jack, you don't have to continue—"

"I spent days hiding so close to them they almost tripped over me. Eventually they gave up and moved on. I was lucky enough to find an old man who had lost a son to the GTM. Through him, I managed to contact a friend who helped me get out of Tierra Montañosa into Ecuador without alerting the government. I didn't want anyone to know I was coming. I wanted everyone to think I was dead.

"Anyway, it's over now, I can't change the way things happened, I just have to live with it."

She heard pain in his voice. Regrets. Her fingers flexed in her lap. She wanted to touch him but she didn't.

"So, that's the story. It's over and done with. We'd better get going."

She stared at him a second. It was clear nothing he'd experienced in the last year was really over and done with, but if he wanted to change the subject, she understood.

"What are you going to do while I go into work?" she asked him.

"I'm pretty self-sufficient, Hannah. Is it located here in town?"

"No, it's about five miles inland. Turn at the second light you come to and go straight. I'll tell you when to turn again."

Traffic was minimal. Jack turned at the light and then followed the twists and turns of the shortcut Hannah used each day to get through town the fastest way.

"Tell me about the foundation," he said as they rumbled over the train tracks.

She brushed her hair away from her eyes. "Santi Correa was born in Peru but spent his youth in several South American countries, including Tierra Montañosa. After college in the States, he taught at a university for a while, got tired of being poor and took a job in the private sector where he was amazingly successful. When he got tired of making money, he started a non-profit organization to develop schools all through South America."

"You're giving me the stuff in the foundation brochure," Jack said as he pulled the car over on a wide spot. From that vantage point, the vista of the small valley included the complex that comprised the foundation's headquarters.

"Santi didn't believe in investing money in appearances when it could be put to good use building schools elsewhere," she added. "Under his direction, things got a little run-down, but since Hugo took over, maintenance has improved." It was true—the buildings now sparkled with a new coat of white paint.

"Of course, part of this is in preparation for the foundation's thirtieth anniversary open house," she continued. "The governor is coming and a congressman or two. As Hugo Correa points out, the more prosperous an enterprise appears, the bigger the donations."

"So, Santi Correa handed over the reins to his son after the incident at Costa del Rio," Jack mused, his thoughts apparently running along the same lines as hers.

"Hugo's abduction and ransom completely gutted poor old Santi. You can't imagine what it was like the day of the ambush. Hugo had insisted Santi skip the morning festivities because Santi had spent a troubled night with his stomach, so the poor old guy felt guilty he hadn't been there. It was just him and me left at the hotel—everyone else had disappeared into oblivion or so it seemed. He stepped down when Hugo and Harrison were returned, and the board voted Hugo in. Santi seemed to age ten years."

"I just met him briefly, but he has to be getting on, doesn't he? Hugo looks like he's in his fifties."

"I think Santi is almost eighty. I know he's failing. Poor Hugo must be broken up about it."

Jack nodded without speaking.

"Why do you look like that?" she demanded.

"Like what?"

"Like you don't agree with me. You don't still think Hugo was involved—"

Jack interrupted her with one of his casual shrugs. "Maybe he wasn't, *cariño*. On the other hand, he's the big shot here now, right? And because of him, his father wasn't involved in any danger."

She sighed. "You don't give up, do you?"

"I gave up thinking you were a bad guy," he said, eyes glittering.

"You do realize you're all over the map, don't you?"

"What do you mean?"

"Well, let's see. First you thought I set up the ambush. Then you thought there was something or someone corrupt within the Staar Foundation. Now you're suggesting Hugo set up the ambush to get himself kidnapped so that his father would turn over the foundation."

"Makes me sound a little schizoid, doesn't it?" he said agreeably.

"Yes."

"If Hugo sympathizes with the GTM, then getting control of the foundation makes sense, doesn't it? If he knows about the schools? If he's diverting funds?"

"I don't know," she said wearily, but she simply couldn't accept Hugo as a bad guy of that magnitude. Besides, Jack didn't know about David. She needed to grow a backbone and tell him about that, but not before she looked inside the gym bag hidden away in her file cabinet.

Anyway, Jack hadn't seen Hugo lying all broken up in the hospital after the ambush....

"So what now?" she added. "You just going to go in there and start poking around?"

"Of course not. Most of the people who work here don't know my face, but Hugo and Harrison Plumber do. If one of them is the inside guy, he might have heard from the rebels that I escaped, but he won't expect me to show up here. I'll save that for a good occasion. For now, I just wanted to get a feel for the place. It's bigger than I imagined."

"It sprawls. And since it's often foggy on the coast, the airstrip here provides a buffer against the weather."

"I thought the Staar Foundation was nonprofit."

"It is."

"It looks pretty posh."

Hannah looked down at the complex and tried to see it through Jack's eyes. From a distance and viewed from above, it did look impressive. Up closer he would see the signs of age, but all and all, he was right, it was a well-run and -managed organization. "The land belonged to the heiress Santi married fifty-five years ago. She donated most of it to the foundation for their headquarters. There's a small adjoining parcel with a family residence on it that stayed in the family. Since Santi moved to the San Francisco area, Hugo took over the house."

"So Santi Correa is a wealthy man."

"More or less. That's another reason why you're wrong about Hugo. He has family money."

"For one thing, that's his father's money, not his," Jack said. "And for another, I didn't say Hugo was in it for money."

"Then what?"

"Like I said before, maybe he sympathizes with the guerillas. How many people work here?"

"It changes. Right now, fifty-one, including me. I'm in charge of public relations and event coordination and then we have positions in fundraising, technology, plus there are classrooms for training seminars and teaching programs as well as office staff and accountants. One of those buildings is a guest dorm. Then there's a cafeteria/lunchroom and a garage for foundation vehicles and the mechanic and maintenance crew that oversees things. They're all good people, Jack."

"And a pilot?"

"Yes, but that's a part-time position as the pilot isn't needed every day. The corporate jet is kept here and when someone needs to use it, they call the pilot."

"Who used to be David. Helicopter, right?"

"Helicopter at first, then he got his pilot's license."

"And that road we just traveled. Is that the road he rode his bike on when he came to work?"

"And the road he was killed on, yes. He'd been called in that morning to take Harrison Plumber down to the city for a meeting concerning the upcoming trip."

"So how did Harrison get to his meeting?"

She opened her mouth and then closed it. "I guess I don't know. Maybe he canceled. Why?"

"Just curious. And the accident happened almost a month before the trip where you and I met—"

"Yes," she said.

"What about the hostages who were killed? Were they all local?"

"Just one. The others were employees from the two schools we'd already opened down there."

"Las personas gastables," Jack said softly.

"What does that mean?"

"The expendable people. The ones not covered by the insurance policy."

"Hostage insurance is extremely expensive in places like Colombia and Tierra Montañosa. It's not unusual for corporations to insure just the top layer. And you shouldn't think anyone was satisfied with the outcome."

He made a sound in his throat. She could practically hear him thinking that someone was because someone had helped plan it. "Are you sure you don't want to go inside?" she added. "Fran Baker is the head of human resources. She's been here twelve years and knows everything. I don't have to use your real name."

"I'll leave her to you. Correa and Plumber must have seen me on the marches between camps. I know I saw them." With mention of his captivity, he seemed to grow restless, turning away from the sight of the foundation.

"If you're still here in a week, you could try attending the Founder's Day open house with a disguise or something."

"Maybe," he said.

"After you drop me off in the parking lot, drive back up here and you'll be out of sight. I'll leave my cell phone and call when I'm ready for you to come get me."

"If I'm right, someone in that building threw a rock through your window last night. That means someone is very aware of you and your actions." He got out of the car and so did she. They met halfway around.

Gripping her arms, he leaned close. "I know why you're going in today, it's written all over your face. If you want to ask questions, go for it, but don't assume anyone is innocent, okay?"

"Jack—"

"You keep the car and your phone. I'll stay up here, I'll watch for you. Just behave normally."

"Good grief, Jack. What are you going to do up here in the weeds for an hour?"

"Cariño," he said, brushing his lips across her forehead. "It's nice to know you care." And then he seemed to fade into the undergrowth.

"Don't flatter yourself," she called, but he was gone.

Chapter Five

The Staar Foundation logo, a big seven-pointed star made of copper, bright gold and polished stainless steel, dominated the foyer. A young male secretary sat at a crescent-shaped desk placed under the star. Recognizing Hannah, he waved her through right as the phone at his elbow rang.

She passed through double doors into a long hallway that led past three offices before her own. Her goal was to avoid seeing anyone—she wanted to get in and out. Jack's words had unnerved her, which annoyed the hell out of her. She'd been working here for six years and this was the first time walking down the hall seemed dangerous and risky and scary and it was Jack's fault.

"Hannah?"

She started even as she recognized the voice and turned to look into Fran Baker's office. As the head of human resources, Fran kept track of everyone and now she screwed up her elfin face. "You don't work today. Everything okay?"

"Yes, yes," Hannah said. "Everything is good."

"Don't lie to me, Hannah Marks," Fran said, smiling. A second later, when her famous radar went into action, she searched Hannah's face and her smile faded. She put down the pen she'd been writing with and stood up.

Fran was five or six years older than Hannah, tiny and compact, always dressed perfectly in clothes that looked as though they'd walked off a runway.

"Did you get another flat on the way home?" Fran said, coming around her desk. The top of her bleached and perfectly coiffed head reached Hannah's shoulder. After looking up at Jack all morning, looking down at the diminutive Fran took a little getting used to. "I knew I should have followed you," Fran continued. "I knew I shouldn't have let you drive off with the spare on the car and no backup. It's dangerous enough being a woman alone nowadays. They still haven't caught the creep who killed those two gals and for all we know, he flattened their tires and followed them home and shot them—"

"Calm down," Hannah said. "There's never been any mention of flat tires in the newspaper articles. I didn't get another flat and no mass murderer bothered me. I just had a mishap. Some kids put a little bomb in the back of my car and—"

"What!"

It took ten minutes to lead Fran through a blow-by-blow account of the car bomb. No way was Hannah going to take the time to start explaining about the shattered window.

"I have to make some copies of papers I lost because of the bomb and then I have to get home to Aubrielle. My grandmother has plans. I'll see you later, Fran."

Fran waved her off though it was obvious she would have loved further details. Hannah traveled the rest of the hallway without incident, but that feeling of being watched was back and she turned once to check behind her. The hall was empty except for the receptionist, who waved as he entered Fran's office with a note in his hand.

"Jack Starling," Hannah muttered under her breath, "I have you to blame for this."

In her office, she closed the door. The key to the bottom drawer of the file cabinet was on the ring with her other work keys, and she dug them out of her purse. The drawer opened silently. The edge of the blue gym bag showed from under a stack of manuals for the new printer and fax machines. Once she had it, she looked inside. As she'd vaguely recalled, there was nothing there but one small piece of paper.

She took it out and as she did so, the outer door opened, causing Hannah to jerk and drop the paper.

Harrison Plumber stood there, watching the scrap flutter to the pristine surface of Hannah's desk. "Oh. I didn't know you came in today," he said, tearing his eyes away from the paper.

Hannah slipped the gym bag under her desk, very aware that Harrison watched her every move. She ignored the paper. "Just for a minute or two. Can I help you, Mr. Plumber?"

Harrison Plumber always struck Hannah as one of those men who seemed lost in an adult-sized body. Since his capture and subsequent release by the GTM, he'd become even more awkward. The intestinal illness he'd returned with had knocked him off his feet and put him in the hospital for weeks.

"I need an envelope," he said, "and my secretary is out. I don't know where to find anything around here. Isn't that pathetic?"

Hannah laughed politely as Harrison shook his balding head. "What size do you need?"

"Legal size. Do you have any of those with the foundation's embossed address?"

She opened a desk drawer and took out a half dozen. "Sure, here."

He stepped closer and took them, stared at her desk-top for a second, then abruptly left.

Hannah looked down to see what, if anything, was written on the paper and if it was facing up. Sure enough, it was, the handwriting clearly visible in black ink. *9D 125 1-2*. The numbers and single letter made no sense to Hannah. They hadn't a year before and they didn't now. She scooped up the paper and tucked it in her pocket, relocked the drawer, and with Jack's cautionary words echoing in her head, took the time to go down the hall and use the copy machine. Then she hurried out of the office, called a hearty goodbye to Fran and drove away, her gut in a giant knot she couldn't explain.

Wait—oh, yes she could.

Jack.

As HANNAH CLICKED OFF HER cell phone from her second call to her grandmother to check on her baby, Jack set the basket of fish and chips he'd just retrieved from the take-out counter on the table in front of her. She'd directed him here, to Noyo Harbor, claiming he had to be hungry after a breakfast of burned toast. He knew she was stalling, and he was willing to play along to a certain point because she was right, he *was* hungry.

Tucked in among fish-processing plants and the fleet, which had obviously seen more prosperous days, were a few small carry-out restaurants, this one with a single picnic table set on a concrete slab above the river. Off to the west, the bay emptied into the ocean; to the east, the river continued inland to a small marina. Overhead, a bridge connected the south shore with the north.

The cold Pacific wind lifted his too-long hair. The odors of sea and humanity were fresh and vibrant, and the sea lions—warming themselves on the floating docks—added comic relief. Best of all, every single thing about the place was two and a half worlds away from the jungles of Tierra Montañosa.

And the food. Sizzling golden-brown deep-fried cod, coleslaw and shoestring fries. Good-for-the-soul kind of grub. The woman sitting at the table made the whole thing, well, one of those moments.

That was another trick he'd learned during his captivity. Freeze a moment. Capture it. Hold on to it. Bring it out later to savor, to taste, to relive, make it a light in the darkness of forever. Damn poetic thoughts for a bodyguard, sure, but things like the look of a raindrop on an orchid glimpsed weeks earlier had seen him through a beating or two.

He sat down opposite Hannah with his own basket of goodies, squeezed on the lemon and took a bite.

Across from him, Hannah smiled wistfully. "You look like a man who's found heaven."

He nodded, too busy eating to talk. She daintily dabbed her fish in tartar sauce while he started on the fries.

He finished long before her, and under the guise of staring at a sailboat motoring past, watched Hannah play around with her food. She was apparently too hyper to enjoy her meal but he remembered the first time they'd met—over a bowl of Tierra Montañosa's signature bar food, grilled fish cubes with garlic and herbs. Back then she'd eaten with gusto and kept up with him when it came to the local brew. She must not have known she was pregnant at the time if she was comfortable drinking booze. Even he knew women didn't do that anymore.

She pushed away the basket at last and he cleared the debris. When he came back, he walked around to her side and perched on the table next to where she sat, his feet on the bench. She looked up at him and despite the wind whipping between them, the air crackled with mutual awareness.

At least he hoped it was mutual.

She pushed herself to her feet and sat back down on the table next to him, her leg brushing his.

He said, "Are you ready to tell me how it went at your office and exactly who you've been protecting?"

She pleated the hem of her jacket as she mumbled, "The office was fine. The only trouble was dealing with all the scary thoughts you planted in my head."

So that's why she'd been so edgy since driving back up that hill—she was pissed at him. "Why did you really go in today, Hannah?"

After a moment, she said, "It ties in to what I'm going to tell you about David."

"David? Is he who you've been protecting?"

She glanced up at him. "I know he's dead—"

"But he's the father of your baby," he finished for her. Did that mean her feelings for David ran deeper than he thought they did or was she protecting her child's father's reputation? It didn't matter, he had no reason to be jealous of a dead man.

"I just want to say that David claimed he never went to Tierra Montañosa, so that means he was never in Costa del Rio, so my suspicions are really dumb."

"That's quite an opener," he said. "I feel a 'but' coming on."

She met his gaze. "*But* he did travel right before his death. He went on a vacation."

"Where?"

"He said he went to Arizona to see a sister and her family."

"You sound dubious."

She looked down at her hands, which she'd folded together and wedged between her knees. As her skirt had hiked up when she sat, the material now molded her thighs while her knees and the rest of her legs were bare. The sight of all that ivory flesh almost undid him so he raised his gaze and tried to keep his thoughts on target.

"I had no reason to doubt him until yesterday when you started asking me about money," she said. "Your accusations made me think of the night David returned from his vacation. He came to my place all excited. He gave me a gym bag with one of those plastic cable ties securing the zipper. He made me swear I would tell no one I had it and I haven't, not until right now."

"You didn't know what was in it?"

"Not until after he died. I opened it then. It was stuffed with money."

"How much money?"

"Fifty thousand dollars in big bills."

Jack whistled. "That's a hunk of change."

"Yes, it is, especially for David. He spent money as fast as he got it."

Jack nodded. That's exactly how he remembered David. The guy loved money and wasn't above pushing the strict limits of the law to get it. "Do you have any idea where the money came from?"

She twisted her head to meet his gaze again, her green eyes almost the same color as the harbor water below them. "No. He was acting kind of strange so I told him he better not be asking me to do something illegal, and he swore he wasn't and that he'd come back the next day and take it back. He said he trusted me."

"But the next day he was killed riding his bike out to the foundation."

"Yes."

"And you didn't find that suspicious?"

"The police investigation ruled David's death was an accident. The truck driver was a local guy with kids and he was reportedly torn up about it. That night I opened the bag and found all that money. I couldn't imagine where he'd gotten that kind of stash, but there were a few funny things about it all that made me wonder if he'd stolen it or found it or something."

"What funny things?"

"Well, the trip for one thing. We were going to meet somewhere for a few days, you know, away from this area where we could spend some time together. But he canceled it at the last moment with this story about needing to go see his sister. I was relieved. By then I knew we couldn't go on the way we were and I'd had enough of his secrets. Well, anyway, when he came back from this sudden urgent trip with that much cash, it made me wonder. I didn't see how I could turn it over to his parents or anyone else for that matter."

"Did you spend it?"

This earned him a glare. "Of course not."

"Then where is it?"

"In one of those commercial mail boxes."

"Hannah, let me get this straight. Your boyfriend brings you a wad of dough, asks you to keep it on the QT, gets himself killed the next day, your house is broken into and you don't put it all together?"

"It didn't all happen in quite that orderly a fashion," she said, her voice sharp. She got to her feet and paced off the distance to the iron railing, turning to lean back against it and stare him down.

"He gave me the money, then he died. I waited for someone to mention it—no one did. I even hinted around with his family at his funeral. They obviously knew nothing. I took the bag to work and locked it in my file cabinet and then I transferred it via my briefcase to the rented box. Then I went to Tierra Montañosa and then the ambush happened.

"You can't imagine what it was like back here with Harrison Plumber and Hugo Correa kidnapped and the rest of you held hostage. I'd just met you and then the next day you were gone…it was crazy. And poor old Santi Correa. He hired me straight out of college, he was always kind to me, and I spent a lot of time with him because he was sure they were going to kill his only son. Then my grandfather died, my mother got married again, Hugo and Harrison were freed and through it all, I was throwing up every morning.

"By the time of the break-in at my apartment, I was beyond frazzled. Nothing was stolen, it appeared to be vandals and I was moving in with my grandmother anyway, so, Mr. Know It All, no, I didn't put it all together until yesterday when you asked if I helped the terrorists in exchange for money. That's when I got to thinking, what if David went to Tierra Montañosa instead of Arizona? What if he sold out?"

Jack was quiet for a few minutes before he said, "Did he know about the planned route to the school?"

"He had access to my papers," she said miserably. "It never occurred to me I had to hide things like that from him of all people."

It wouldn't, but if she was right, her baby's father had

helped kill ten people. *David, you raging bastard, how could you do that?*

"If he went out of the country, his passport will be stamped," Jack said.

"I sent his mother a box of things after David died but I don't remember all that was in it."

"Did you talk to his sister at his funeral? I mean, did she mention him visiting?"

"No, she didn't come. Just his mother and stepfather and one brother."

"You could call his sister and think of some reason to ask about his visit last year to Arizona. We could probably rule him out if he was really with her."

"I don't know what excuse I could offer," she said. "They think of me as David's coworker, not his girlfriend."

"You could think of something," he said.

She thought for a moment, then nodded. "Yes, I could think of something." She turned around and stared out at the water and he got up and went to stand beside her. "Did anyone else from the foundation go down several weeks before the school opening and the ambush?"

"You're still trying to pin things on someone who works here," she said.

"I can imagine David having information he'd sell to the guerillas, but I can't quite see how he'd do it all on the sly, especially since he wouldn't have the contacts because he didn't go down there regularly."

"He spoke Spanish because his stepfather is from Mexico. Actually, he understood more than he could say. If someone from the foundation went, too, wouldn't you have been notified to act as their bodyguard?"

"If it was on the up-and-up. If it wasn't..."

She shook her head and looked so burdened by all

this that his heart went out to her. He found it impossible to believe that twenty-four hours before, he'd totally believed she'd set him up and sold all the others down the creek.

"I don't know how this all fits together," he told her, looking down at the sweep of her lashes against her cheeks, "but I think it does. There are two issues. One, who plotted the ambush? If I'm right, someone in the Staar Foundation is diverting funds to the GTM and the GTM is using those funds to finance terrorist training schools. If they're planning some act of terrorism to make their point, can we stop it? And what does any of this have to do with someone threatening you?"

"That's at least three things. The most obvious answer to the last one is that someone knows about the money."

"That explains the break-in, but it doesn't explain the note or the threats. It's almost like there are two different minds at work. You said going into the office tied in to David. How?"

"I almost forgot," she said, reaching into her jacket pocket and extracting a small sheet of paper.

"What's this?" he asked as he read aloud. *"9D 125 1-2."*

"It was in the gym bag with the money," Hannah said. "I have no idea what it means. Do you?"

"Are you kidding? I don't know, maybe a locker or a safety-deposit box, maybe a location, maybe an identity number, maybe nothing. Do you still have the gym bag?"

"It's locked in the file cabinet at work. It's empty now and there's nothing unusual about it."

He handed the paper back, but she waved it away. "No, you keep it."

Folding it carefully, he put it in his wallet.

Hannah sighed, which lifted her breasts a little under her black jacket. Maybe it was a relief for her to have this out in the open, although how they were going to make sense of anything without David to enlighten them was a mystery.

As they leaned side by side against the rail staring down at the water, he became increasingly aware of every detail of her from her hip an inch or two from his to her glistening hair blowing back from her face. When she reached up to rub her eyes and he saw her lashes were moist, he impulsively put an arm around her shoulders. Her whole body stiffened. He was about to take his arm away when she gently relaxed. Because he could not hold back another moment, he kissed the top of her head, inhaling the salty freshness of her hair. She turned to look up at him, eyes registering surprise.

Before she could chew him out, he lowered his face to hers, waiting for her to draw away or warn him off, but she didn't. Instead, she met him halfway and as the cold wind blowing off the water buffeted their clothes, he cupped her cheeks in his hands and claimed her mouth.

She broke the connection and held him away from her for a long, intense moment, then she slowly wrapped her arms around his neck, her fingers linking behind his head, twining in his hair, leaning in against him, her breasts pressing against his chest, her hip against his. She looked so deep and far into his eyes it alarmed him—for a second he felt naked and vulnerable. What was she looking for, what did she see?

It was a relief when her lips touched his, and when her tongue slid against his, fire erupted in his groin, singed his skin, sent smoke out his ears, or at least it felt that way. The year since the last time they made love shattered like crystal; it seemed just a minute ago that he'd stretched out beside her...

If there weren't so damn many layers of clothes between them, he'd— Man, he needed to get a grip. Since when did a kiss or two plunge him into such a frenzy?

He caught her upper arms in his hands and gently pushed her away. She blinked a couple of times and looked surprised. Hell, he was surprised. In his head, he got a stranglehold on his libido and stuffed it into a box. Tight fit.

He didn't know what to tell her, only that he'd fallen into a trap of some sort, he'd lost his focus. A year in the jungle with no sex had given him a one-track mind that this woman ignited every time she looked at him.

But there was more at stake than a roll in the hay. He shrugged, unsure how to say what he didn't want to say.

"I got carried away," she said softly.

"Yeah, well, me, too."

"There's something between us," she said. "I can't deny that."

He swallowed what felt like a starfish. "*Cariño,* you were right last night, you've changed. *We've* changed. I'm your baby's bodyguard, not your lover. You need a man who can be a father and we both know that's not me."

"No, it's not," she said and with such conviction it almost made him mad.

He rubbed his forehead, ran a hand up through his hair and redirected his gaze right into her eyes. "The food, the day, the freedom, you—everything got to me. I should be focusing on David's apparent windfall and the Staar Foundation and who is out to get you, and instead, here I am wanting to take you to bed every time we're alone."

She reached up and ran a hand down his cheek, her touch light and gentle as her fingers grazed his scars. He closed his eyes and wished things were different.

"David was a mistake from start to finish," she said. "You're right. I can't afford to make more mistakes."

"I know," he said, looking down at her again. "It worries me you take the things that have happened to you so lightly. Your grandmother is terrified."

"I know she is. I didn't know how deeply until today." She leaned her head against his chest. It was the kind of thing a person did when they felt familiar and comfortable with another person and it amazed him more than her lusty kiss had.

He tried patting her shoulder. "I really will do my best to keep your baby and grandmother safe." He didn't add that he'd move heaven and earth to keep her safe, too. "I know the Staar Foundation is involved in some way with the GTM and—"

"Jack?" she said, looking up at him. "Forget about everything that's happening to me. Forget about what you think about the Staar Foundation. We have no proof about where David got that money or what anyone else is responsible for, either. Are you sure your suspicions aren't being driven by your need for revenge?"

"No, I'm not sure."

She looked startled by his answer. He added, "I'll be honest. Maybe I do want to see the bastards who slaughtered all those men twist in the wind. Maybe I want the year they stole from me back. Maybe I'm seething inside. But the bottom line is this—I learned a long time ago to listen to my gut."

She nodded as though what he said was reasonable. "I just—"

She stopped as a noise erupted from her purse that she'd left lying on the table. For a tinny little melody playing from within a closed object, it galvanized her in a hurry. She dug through her purse until she found the prize, flipping open the tiny cell phone as she raised it to her ear.

"They hung up," she said, pushing buttons. "It's our home phone. I wonder why Grandma hung up." She pushed another button, apparently dialing her grandmother's house. Her face reflected her tension. Jack felt a knot form in his own stomach just watching her face.

"No answer," she said.

"Did the call go through?"

She checked the screen. "The signal is fine. She just doesn't answer." Her face had lost every drop of color. "We have to go, Jack."

He was already running toward the car.

Chapter Six

Hannah tried calling home numerous times. Then she finally thought to try the number of one of the poker ladies. The phone was answered on the second ring.

"Barb? Thank goodness," Hannah said, sparing Jack a smile of relief. Obviously something had happened to the home phone and her grandmother hadn't thought to borrow a cell from one of the women who were in the house with her and Aubrielle.

"Hello, Hannah, dear, is everything okay?"

Jack had just turned off the road into Allota, passing the grocery store where the car had blown up the day before, then the garage that was trying to put it back together again. "I'm almost at the house," she told Barb. "I got worried when Grandma didn't answer her phone."

"Well, she's there. We all left a good hour ago so Mimi could put the baby down for a nap. I know she wouldn't leave."

"What do you mean she's *there?* You aren't with her?"

"No," Barb said.

"Is anyone?"

"No. Mimi shooed us all away. Jackie and Darlene,

they're sisters you know, well, they got into a little bit of an altercation and it woke the baby...."

"Barb, excuse me, I'll get back to you, okay?"

Hannah folded the phone and looked at Jack. "Grandma is supposedly home and alone with Aubrielle."

"Damn. Okay, two more minutes," he said, taking the next turn with screeching tires.

There were no cars in front of the house and the door was ajar. The Harley was still parked by the side of the garage.

"Don't enter the house," Jack said as Hannah tore open the car door and jumped out. She heard him, but she had no intention of complying. A million thoughts ran through her mind, none of them good.

"Hannah, wait!" Jack yelled. "Maybe she's just outside in the back, maybe the wind blew the door open."

Or maybe she was lying inside with a bludgeoned head. And Aubrielle? Hannah wanted to kick herself for leaving today, for letting Jack leave with her, for leaving her grandmother alone, virtually unprotected, with a three-month-old baby—

"Hannah," she heard Jack yell as she raced through the front door. She stopped abruptly. The place looked like it had been torn apart by a cyclone. "Grandma?" she whispered. "Aubrielle?"

Jack was suddenly beside her. "I don't think they're here but we better look around," he said as he walked past her and pushed open the kitchen door. She looked over his shoulder. The drain board was cluttered with tea cups and little plates, but there was no sign of a search as evidenced in the living room. The back door was wide open. Hannah ducked under Jack's arm and ran outside.

The small yard was clearly visible and totally empty of humans. The back gate swung open on its hinges.

Hannah followed Jack back into the living room. By mutual and silent consent, they hurried down the hall. Jack took Mimi's room as Hannah continued on to the nursery.

This room, too, looked ordinary except for the cordless phone lying on its back by the changing table. Hannah picked it up. Pushing redial, she watched as her cell-phone number flashed on the small screen.

Jack ducked into the room. "Anything?"

"No."

"Check the closet," he said.

She checked the closet.

"Is there anywhere she might go? A neighbor's, maybe?"

"Possibly the Hendrickses' house, but you'd think she'd leave a note and it doesn't explain the condition of the living room. There's no other place here for her to hide except the garage and grandpa's shop. Oh, and the basement."

"She has a basement?"

"Kind of. It's just a small area below a portion of the house where the land sloped. Grandpa created access to it so they could store things."

"And how do you access it?"

"Back here," Hannah said, making her way to the end of the hall, "but Grandma hates it. Too many spiders." She opened the closet door. The two empty suitcases that usually took up floor space had been stacked on one side. Hannah slid a floor panel aside to reveal a dark opening.

The first narrow step leading down was just barely visible in the ambient light from the hall. Lowering her voice to a whisper, she added, "They just used it to store Christmas stuff. There should be a flashlight hanging on the hook to your right."

"No flashlight," he said, lowering his voice, as well. "I saw one in the room I used last night. Wait here."

No flashlight? Since when? As he raced off, Hannah was sure she heard a rustling noise. Heart skipping beats, she grabbed the railing and started down the stairs. It had to be her grandmother who took the flashlight....

A light from below suddenly blinded her. "I have a gun and I'm not afraid to use it," Mimi's voice cried out loud and strong. "Take one more step and I'll blast you to kingdom come."

"It's me, Grandma, it's Hannah."

"Hannah, oh my goodness." The light flicked enough away that Hannah could see where she was going again. Taking the steps as fast as she dared and wondering how in the world her grandmother had made it down here holding a baby, she reached the bottom just as Jack reached the top, a light held before him.

Mimi emerged from a dark corner of the tiny, dank basement, wending her way through old boxes, web-strewn Christmas tree stands and an artificial tree or two. She held Aubrielle clutched tightly against her chest. The light playing out in front of her wavered in her trembling hand, belying the vigor she'd put into her voice a moment before.

Hannah threw both her arms around her grandmother and her baby, knocking the flashlight from Mimi's hand. "Here, sit down," she coaxed, helping the trembling older woman sit on a dusty box. Jack was there in a blink, and he knelt by the older woman as Hannah chased the flashlight's spinning light.

"Are you okay, Mimi?" Jack said.

"I am now," Mimi replied but she still sounded shaky. "When I heard footsteps overhead, I thought they'd come back," she added. Hannah turned in time to see her grandmother clasp a hand to her chest.

"Thought *who* had come back, Grandma?"

Mimi shuddered. "I don't know."

"Let's get you out of here and you can tell us what happened," Jack said. He was the one to lift Aubrielle from Mimi's arms, pausing a second to look down at the baby as he gathered the loose blanket around her slumbering form, tucking it close to her.

A blitzkrieg of sensations sucked the air out of Hannah's lungs at the sight of the big man dressed in black holding the bundle of pink. *Her* bundle of pink. She abruptly sat down next to Mimi.

"Are you all right?" Mimi asked, patting her hand.

Hannah closed her eyes as she mumbled, "No."

"BEFORE THE COPS GET HERE, tell us what happened," Jack said. Hannah had made the call to the police and was now sitting in a kitchen chair nursing Aubrielle. They'd decided to leave the living room as it was until investigators could dust for fingerprints.

Jack settled Mimi into another chair and even poured her a cup from the electric teakettle on the drain board. It was kind of odd to see him comforting the older woman. Hannah hadn't seen him in that role before.

"Jackie was putting something high octane in her tea and told everyone Darlene was going to have liposuction and Darlene got madder than a hatter—oh, dear, don't tell either of them I told you two that, it was a secret. Well, anyway, I kicked them out right after Hannah called and said you'd be starting home pretty soon," Mimi began, glancing at Hannah. "Then I went into the nursery to change Aubrielle. I'd just finished with her diaper when I heard a noise at the door. I knew you two had a key. When the noise went on and on, I got too spooked to go look."

The cup rattled on the saucer as she set it on the table. "I had the phone with me so I called you. I could hear it ringing and then it dawned on me that if you were at the front door, I should hear your phone. When I heard the door make a kind of popping noise and a voice that wasn't either of yours, I really did panic. The phone slipped out of my fingers when I grabbed the baby."

"Oh, Grandma," Hannah said. "I'm so sorry—"

"No, dear, it's my own fault. I should never have sent the girls home. Anyway, I couldn't think of anywhere to hide Aubrielle. She was wide-awake and making little noises, so I started toward the back of the house thinking maybe we could get out the bathroom window and then I remembered I should have retrieved the phone but it was too late. When I heard something break in the living room, I remembered the old basement. I guess the noise out there covered the noise I made opening and closing the linen door."

"So you didn't see anyone?" Hannah said.

"No."

"How about the voice?" Jack asked. "Male or female? More than one?"

"I'm not sure. Someone just yelled, 'Anyone home?'" I didn't say a word, not after the window last night and your warnings this morning. Maybe if I'd been alone I would have been braver. I just slunk away with Aubrielle. The living room is a bloody mess, isn't it? I should have tried to stop whoever it was."

"Furniture and knickknacks can be replaced," Jack said with a quick glance at Hannah. "People can't."

As Mimi worried aloud about photographs, Hannah finished nursing Aubrielle and stood up. She'd heard a car come to a stop and caught a glimpse of flashing lights out front.

"The cops are here," she announced. "Uh, Grandma," she added carefully. "I think we should leave Jack completely out of this."

Jack started to protest.

"I agree," Mimi said, and, shooting to her feet, went to answer the door.

"Hannah," Jack began, but she covered his lips with a finger. Probably not a smart idea. Touching his lips just created a whole lot of other problems. She dropped her hand as though she'd touched a flame.

"You have nothing to do with what is happening here, but you are a stranger with a false identity," she said. "If they get started on you, they may look no further or they may make a connection to the foundation and if you're right about what's going on out there, whoever is responsible might go underground. You wanted me to take all this seriously. Well, I finally am."

"Hannah," he said, moving the blanket aside to uncover Aubrielle's face, "I'm *her* bodyguard. I'm not going anywhere."

"Be reasonable, Jack. Do what's best for her. The police will be here for heaven's sake."

He stared into her eyes for a count of five. "The Harley is in the side yard. People have undoubtedly seen me coming and going."

"I'll tell them you're a visiting friend. They accepted you as that yesterday. We'll just leave you out of last night's rock through the window and today's break-in. Just go out the back door and walk down to the beach. Leave it to me. I'll come find you later."

"No. Don't leave your grandmother or the baby. I won't be far."

And then, as he was proving he did very efficiently, he disappeared out the back door and through the gate.

JACK EASILY DODGED THE policeman outside while doing his best not to compromise any evidence the fleeing intruder may have left in his or her wake. There was no way he was going to get out of sight of the house, however, so the trick was to find somewhere he could watch what was going on without being seen.

This he did by skirting an old car that had been abandoned across the street in a vacant lot, taking cover in an even older shed close to collapse. Through the dirty, cracked window, he watched as the police did all the forensic work. One man stood at the door for quite a while talking to Mimi and Hannah. Before long, Mimi wandered off with the baby in her arms and Hannah stayed at the door, leaning against the frame, smiling and touching her luscious strawberry-gold hair while the officer chatted up a blue streak.

The cop finally turned around and started toward the squad car where his partner, an older guy, had retreated sometime before and seemed to be doing paperwork. Jack recognized the younger man as the policeman from the night before, the one who had given Hannah a ride home. As she closed the front door, the officer took a quick look over his shoulder, and when he looked back at the car, he had a stupid grin on his face.

Jack looked down for a second as a tightening in his rib cage caught his attention. Must be the fried fish.

Once the police car pulled away, he let himself out the broken door through which he'd entered, and, walking the long way around, once again approached Mimi's house. He found both women in the living room working on cleaning up yet another mess and pitched in to help. As they worked, they told him everything the police had said but there was little that would help.

"Officer Latimer said he'd take the note and turn it in to the detectives down in Fort Bragg. The local station isn't set up for much in the way of investigating."

"They acted like we knew what it was all about and weren't telling," Mimi said as she sprayed a table with furniture polish to wipe off the fingerprint dust.

"I don't think they did," Hannah said. "I think they were just as confused as we are."

"Did they lift any prints?" Jack asked.

"A few," Hannah said. "They took samples of mine and Mimi's and asked that you stop by the station to give them a sample of yours."

"I should have expected that," Jack said.

"I told them I wasn't sure when you would return and gave them the water glass in the bathroom you used this morning so they could get your prints to rule them out from the ones they collected."

"Good thinking," Jack said.

"She watches those shows on TV," Mimi explained.

"They didn't find any shoe prints or tire tracks," Hannah continued. "And like before, nothing seems to be missing."

"Maybe they were looking for cold, hard cash," Jack said with a meaningful look at Hannah.

Mimi laughed. "In this house? Good luck. I think it was probably some drug addict up from the city."

"Maybe," Hannah said. "Officer Latimer said he'd get back to me about what they find, if anything."

Jack came close to asking what took Latimer so long

to say goodbye at the door but stopped himself. It was none of his damn business.

HANNAH WAS UP EARLY THE NEXT morning. She'd spent the afternoon before doing her best to catch up on work, but there were details for the rapidly approaching festivities that needed to be addressed from the office.

Working from home had its distractions, the primary one being Aubrielle. Hannah could never spend enough time with her. If it wasn't for the paycheck, she would happily have quit her job for a couple of years; thankfully, she had her grandmother, who loved Aubrielle as much as she did.

And now there was the conundrum of Jack. He couldn't go snoop at the office because they might figure out who he was. That meant he had to protect the home front, and that meant he had to spend time with Mimi and Aubrielle, right exactly where Hannah didn't want him.

It made sense that the only way to get Jack out of their lives was to figure out what was going on. Then they wouldn't need a bodyguard anymore and Jack could go about doing whatever it was he needed to go about doing. Like leaving.

She dressed quickly after taking care of Aubrielle, laying the baby back in the crib for a morning nap. By the time she walked into the kitchen, she'd put on her game face. What she found was a replay of the morning before. Everyone in the house seemed to be an early riser lately.

"Baby is fed, cuddled, changed and back in her crib," she told her grandmother as she kissed the older woman's wrinkled cheek. She was relieved to see some color back in Mimi's face.

Jack sat at the table, gamely eating more burned toast and a crusty scrambled egg. He looked her over, his gaze lingering on her tight reddish-brown slacks.

"Workday?" he said.

She poured hot coffee into a travel mug and grabbed a granola bar from the cupboard. "Yep. I'll be home early this afternoon. The glass people are coming at noon to actually replace the window, right Grandma?"

Mimi peeked over the paper. "Right."

Jack had fixed the lock on the front door the night before, so once the window was replaced, the house would be secure again. Well, as secure as any house could be. Hannah was beginning to suspect security was an illusion.

"I took a walk around the neighborhood this morning," Jack said. "I didn't see anything suspicious."

"Well, Grandma, I guess I have to borrow your car again. At least we got the groceries yesterday."

"Meat loaf tonight," Mimi announced. "And I'm going to make strawberry preserves out of the early crop berries we bought yesterday."

Jack said, "My favorite." It was unclear whether he was referring to meat loaf or jam. Of course, he had no idea what damage Mimi could do to either one of those.

Hannah used the back door as Jack had insisted the car be locked in the garage at night. She wasn't surprised to hear footsteps following and turned as Jack caught up to her.

"I'll call the garage for you, if you like."

"Okay."

"I hate you going out there alone."

She continued walking. The sooner she got to work, the sooner she could come home. "I'm okay."

"Remember, don't be careless. Don't ask leading questions that will alert—"

"Jack? Stop." She poked his chest. "*You* bodyguard for Aubrielle—" and then poking herself added "—*me* intrepid office worker. You take care of my grandmother and baby today, that's your job."

"Anything I need to know about my client?"

She shook her head at him. "She likes to be rocked and sung to but don't worry, Grandma can do all the nurturing, you just look out the window and shoot bad guys."

He saluted.

"No, really, Jack, just keep Aubrielle safe. You know, from a distance."

JACK STARLING WAS GETTING MORE entwined in her life by the moment and that put an urgency on finding some answers. Avoiding contact with everyone, Hannah managed to get to her office and spent the next hour or so going through anything about the Tierra Montañosa schools she could find. There was tons of information on the Internet. It was trying to figure out what was and wasn't important that was the tricky part.

Like she'd told Jack, she knew the foundation's background. She knew Santi Correa had vowed to make sure there were at least three schools in the small country to counteract the poverty and drug-related trade that robbed youth of their future. It was impossible to imagine Santi involved with the GTM.

That left Hugo and Harrison Plumber. Both had suffered grievously at the hands of the GTM. No matter what Jack said, they seemed equally unlikely to be involved.

What if it had been David? What if he'd had an

accomplice and that accomplice was now looking for the money? But why threaten Hannah when, to her knowledge, she was doing nothing to challenge a single soul?

There was a rap on her door and Fran stuck her head in. She quickly looked back out into the hall, then slipped inside.

Hannah closed the program she'd been running on the computer as she said, "Is something wrong?"

Fran settled herself in Hannah's visitor chair. "You will not believe what I just heard. Steel yourself, it's about you."

"Me?"

Her voice dropped lower. "It's about your love life and it's juicy."

All Hannah could think of was that someone had figured out who Jack was and where he was currently living.

She braced herself for the worst.

Chapter Seven

Fran's eyes twinkled as she spoke. "I don't know who started it," she said softly, "I just overheard it in the coffee room. Two gals from maintenance were talking to each other." Her voice dropped another decibel as she added, "One of them said you and David Lengell had an affair before he died."

Fran sat back in her chair, her eyes never leaving Hannah's face. As far as Hannah was aware, Jack was the only one who knew she'd been dating David. He'd hardly had the time, opportunity or inclination to tell anyone about this....

Fran apparently misread Hannah's silence. "Don't get me wrong, I know it's not true. If I see them again—"

"Even if it was true," Hannah interrupted, "what would it matter? David is dead."

"It matters because if Hugo Correa gets wind you conducted an intra-office romance against company policy, it could jeopardize your job. And let me remind you, hon, I know all about the Frenchman down in Costa del Rio who fathered Aubrielle, but most of the people here don't. If the rumor about you and David spreads, then it's not a big jump to imagine it ending up with David as Aubrielle's father."

See? Hannah's conscience shouted in her ear. *This*

*is where lying gets you. This is where sneaking around
gets you.* But it was too late. If the rumor was circulat-
ing, then people would reach whatever conclusions they
wanted. But what if this news reached David's parents?
She did not want to hurt them.

Damn. Her biggest regret was having a relationship with David in the first place. At the time, it hadn't
seemed like that big a deal. He'd argued the policy was
outdated, she'd agreed.

"Please don't talk to anyone about this," she told Fran.
"Let it die."

"I don't get you. Why would you—"

"Fran, there's a lot going on right now. You don't know
all of it. A rumor or two is the least of my concerns."

Fran narrowed her dark eyes and tapped a finger
against Hannah's desktop. "Okay, missy, what's up? Tell
me everything."

No way was Hannah telling Fran everything, but the
break-in and the broken window were now common
knowledge and it was even possible Officer Latimer
or one of the other policemen would come out to the
foundation to ask questions. Also, if someone here was
doing these terrible things, then maybe having it out in
the open was the way to go. So, Hannah told Fran about
all the scares she and her grandmother had experienced
in the last two days, leaving Jack and his suspicions
concerning the foundation out of it.

She also omitted any mention of David's money,
though for a moment or two she was tempted to admit
she'd dated him. On the other hand she could think of
no way that information could help and a couple of ways
it might work against her.

"I can't believe you're going through all this," Fran
said when Hannah finished. "And you really have no

idea what this person wants in your house or thinks you're doing to them?"

"None. If they're trying to scare me to death, they're doing a good job of it."

Fran nodded thoughtfully. "It's like it's two different people."

That was exactly what Jack had said the day before— two minds. Chills skittered between Hannah's shoulder blades. One person having it in for her was bad enough.

"If I hear anything at all, I'll tell you, okay?" Fran said, her eyes earnest.

"That would be wonderful. But don't alert people, don't set yourself in anyone's sights, okay?"

"Me?" Fran laughed. "Everyone talks to me, hon, you know that." Her expression got serious and she lowered her voice again. "All this aside, I'm going to be truthful with you, Hannah. I simply don't believe you."

"You don't believe me? What do you mean? You don't believe that someone threw a rock through my grandmother's window or came into her house—"

"No, I believe all that. I don't think you're telling the truth about you and David."

"I didn't say anything about David."

"I know. You've been very careful not to comment on David at all. However, I'm remembering a couple of times when he came in to shoot the breeze with me and kept staring down here toward your office. And there was that time I thought I saw his car at your house, only you told me it wasn't, and another when you were both at the theatre. I'm beginning to think the ladies I overheard were telling the truth and that the reason you want me to drop it is because you know it."

Fran's face reflected the enjoyment she got out of

knowing other people's business. In retrospect, it seemed amazing to Hannah that Fran hadn't figured out she and David were seeing one another long before. "Fran, will you please just let this drop?"

"I just like to have my facts straight." She bit the inside of her lip and added, "Did David ever give you anything?"

Hannah very cautiously said, "What do you mean?"

"Oh, you know. If you guys were so close, it must be comforting to have something special of his."

Was she hinting around about Aubrielle? "I don't know what you're talking about," she said.

"Touchy, touchy," Fran said, laughing.

"Listen, Fran—"

"Forget it," Fran said. "I was just curious. You know me."

Hannah was beginning to wonder if she did.

JACK HAD NEVER SPENT SO MUCH time with an elderly lady and a baby. Of the two, the baby was the easier to get along with. He'd noticed the way Hannah hadn't included her grandmother in any of their—okay, his—suspicions about the foundation; given the older woman's propensity for talking without thinking, he appreciated that, but it made answering her questions a little tricky.

The baby, on the other hand, couldn't utter a single sensible word nor did she seem to understand any and in a strange way, he found that kind of refreshing. The kid had mastered living in the moment and he admired that.

What he was having the most difficulty with was not being in the middle of things. When he'd pushed his way into Hannah's life by volunteering to be Aubrielle's bodyguard, he hadn't understood how much downtime would be involved. Even his Zen-like exercises couldn't help calm the anxiety roiling in his gut.

Mimi must have noticed how impatient he was feeling, for she presented him with the stroller and suggested a walk. No way he was pushing a pink stroller around town. She promptly produced an alternative, a sling-type thing that could be strapped around him with the baby inside it. That had possibilities. A few minutes later, he'd strapped the baby to his chest and pulled on a jacket. Mimi, who had been unable to find her canning jars and so hadn't been able to make her jam, agreed to be escorted to the neighbor's house where she promised to stay until he came for her.

On foot, he made his way down to the repair garage and found out Hannah's car would be ready in two days. He also spied a truck he could trade his Harley for and made a deal for the guys to bring the truck out later that day. Then he walked to a restaurant where he ordered a toasted sesame seed bagel slathered with cream cheese that was blessedly free of any charred bits, and ate it standing up as Aubrielle gazed at him with deep blue eyes.

"Aubrielle is an awful big name for a little shrimp like you," he told her as he brushed a crumb or two off her forehead. "I'm going to call you Abby. Better not tell your mom."

They all got back to the house in time to let the glass guys in. Jack could think of no way to get around eating the "well-done" grilled cheese sandwich Mimi presented. Stuffed and bored beyond endurance, he agreed to go back down into the nasty little excuse for a basement and check for Mimi's canning jars. It seemed extremely unlikely that anything bad could happen to the baby or her grandmother as they watched the glass people install the new front window.

Every box in the basement held old Christmas ornaments and decorations. There were enough garlands, felt stockings and twinkling lights to cover every surface of the house but there were no jars. He was in the attic checking out the piles of bags and trunks up there when Hannah appeared at the top of the ladder. A weak shaft of sunlight hit her face as she called out to him, illuminating her reddish-gold hair, making her look like a blushing angel.

Damn, he needed to get out of this house, away from all these females.

"Find the jars?" she asked.

"Nope. I'm beginning to think your grandmother is imagining them."

"No, I've seen them around somewhere, maybe when I was moving my stuff in a few months ago. Give me a minute or two to think about it."

"What about work? Did you find out anything helpful?"

Her brow creased for a second but she shook her head.

"Hannah, what aren't you telling me?"

"Nothing."

"Damn it," he snarled, getting to his feet and walking to the ladder opening. "I've been stuck here all day spinning my wheels. What the hell happened out at the foundation?"

She shook her head, bit her lip and said, "Really, nothing. Nothing important, anyway. Right now there's another matter to resolve—"

"Oh, yes, I almost forgot, the great mystery of the missing canning jars."

"I am referring," she snarled back, "to the great mystery of a guy named Hank Nebbins who is currently downstairs claiming you're trading your Harley for an ugly green truck. Is that true?"

"I can't take Aubrielle anywhere on a bike," he said.

"Where do you plan on taking Aubrielle?" she asked, brow furrowing.

She was obviously unhappy about the prospect of him transporting her daughter. "I don't have the slightest idea but it's good to be prepared," he said.

"I wouldn't want you to lose your Harley because of my baby—"

"Hannah? It's a bike. It's a thing. It's more fun than some rides, but at the end of the day, that's what it is, a ride."

"That's very evolved of you," she said, with arched eyebrows, making it very clear she thought he was full of it. She preceded him down the ladder. He followed, enjoying the occasional glimpse of her milky cleavage to say nothing of the flare of her hips.

Evolved. Yep, that was him. He flashed to the afternoon they'd kissed. He suddenly wished he could snatch back the lost opportunity. Why had he gotten all noble? Give him the chance and he'd show her how evolved he was....

Okay, okay, he was frustrated, that's all. He'd spent the day accomplishing nothing, getting nowhere, stuck babysitting while a clock ticked off the minutes and now his supposed partner in honor, truth and the American way was getting all evasive.

Something had to give. Soon.

EVERY ONCE IN A WHILE, Aubrielle evoked her infant privilege of fussing and that afternoon was one of them. While her grandmother walked the crying baby, Hannah finally recalled the baby swing a friend had passed along weeks before. She knew exactly where it was, too, on the top shelf of the closet in the room Jack was using. Her hands had no more closed around the swing when the crying stopped and her grandmother tiptoed down the hall past the door, carrying the now-exhausted baby in her arms.

The act of digging through the closet had reminded Hannah where she'd seen her grandmother's canning jars, too. She was moving boxes when Jack came into the room, the transaction with the truck apparently concluded.

"What are you up to?" he asked.

"I'm looking for my grandmother's jars. I think I saw them in this closet when I was storing some of my stuff after the move."

He sat on the edge of the futon, got to his feet and paced the floor. His lurking presence began to get on her nerves. She set aside a small sealed box to get to the larger, more promising-looking one beneath it.

"I think I found them," she said.

"What's this?" Jack asked. As she pulled out the box of jars, she looked over her shoulder. He'd picked up the smaller box.

"I don't know—"

"It's addressed to Donna Gonzales. Isn't that David's mother?" He turned it to show Hannah the label she'd affixed months before. Hannah had obviously moved the box from her apartment to the house instead of mailing it.

"Yeah, she has a different last name than David. I thought I'd sent it. No wonder she never responded. I'd better get it off tomorrow—"

"After what you told me about David's stash? Maybe there's something we can use in this box. At least we could look."

"I guess," she said, racking her brain to recall what she'd put in the box. The trouble was she'd been several months pregnant, her house had just been burglarized and they'd just buried her grandfather. She'd been so frazzled that there were lots of things she had done at the time she could barely recall doing now. There'd also been all the people from work who had helped her move. In retrospect, she supposed it was inevitable things got mixed up.

Mimi spoke from the doorway. "Aubrielle's down for a nap so we don't need the swing now. Oh, are those my jars?"

"Yes," Hannah said, dragging the big box out of the closet.

Mimi came into the room to look in the box, then she turned her attention to Jack. "I have to ask you, Jack, how did Aubrielle get sesame seeds in her hair?"

"Sesame seeds?" Hannah said.

Jack looked a little embarrassed. "I had a snack when we were out walking. A seed must have fallen off a bagel. Sorry."

"Oh, it's no big deal, I just wondered," Mimi said with a warm smile.

"You went walking with my baby?" Hannah said. "When?"

"Today."

"Why?"

"It was that or go stir-crazy. I think she liked it."

Mimi laughed, but Hannah felt her blood chill. She did not like the idea of Jack getting that comfortable with Aubrielle. *Well, of course he'll get comfortable with her, just as she'll get comfortable with him.*

"That baby will have you wrapped around her finger before you know it," Mimi said, patting Jack's shoulder. "Would you carry the jars into the kitchen for me?"

"Sure," he said, and, leaning down, lifted the box from Hannah's lap. "I'll be right back," he said with a meaningful glance at the smaller box.

The box and what it held suddenly seemed a lot less worrisome than Jack Starling. He'd traded his bike for a truck, he'd carried her baby around town all afternoon and felt comfortable enough doing it to actually eat with her strapped to his chest, and now her grandmother was domesticating him.

She had to get him out of here.

Jack came back into the room wielding his pocket-knife. Within seconds he had the flaps of the smaller box open and despite her racing thoughts, Hannah got caught up in the mystery of its contents.

"Oh, I remember now," she said as moved aside a layer of tissue paper. "His passport *is* in here. It's in an envelope with a couple of letters from his mother."

Jack lifted out several old music tapes and Hannah smiled when she saw them. "David listened to different music when he did different things. Heavy rock for biking, classical for flying, like that."

"Why did you have them?"

"These are some his brother gave him. He brought them to me because I was the only one he knew who still had an old tape player. I thought his family might want them back."

There were also a couple of VCR tapes in the box,

one of David's first solo landing when he got his pilot's license and another of a cousin's wedding.

A large envelope was tucked underneath a knit cap and a couple of dog-eared paperbacks David had lent her. Hannah carefully removed a handful of photos, none of them with her in them—those she'd kept—two letters and the passport. She handed the passport to Jack, who opened it and scanned the pages.

"Well?" she said.

"He's got a stamp for Ecuador," Jack said.

"When is it dated?"

"Thirteen months ago. The twenty-eighth of April."

"When he said he was in Arizona."

"Ecuador is very close to Tierra Montañosa."

"Yes," she said. "He lied. He could very well have gone over the border—"

"Or met someone in Ecuador. Someone from the GTM. But he'd need an accomplice from the Staar Foundation."

She was about to protest but didn't. He was right. Everything she knew about David pointed to the fact he would need someone else setting things up. For one thing, he didn't speak Spanish well.

For the first time, she really believed her old boyfriend had sold out his company and been responsible for multiple deaths.

And that someone else she knew had helped him.

Chapter Eight

"We need to find out if anyone else from the Staar Foundation traveled to Ecuador a year ago April. Do you remember?" Jack demanded. He'd gotten to his feet and was pacing the cluttered room.

"No. As far as I know, no one did. I'm not sure how I can find out if someone wants to keep it a secret."

"What about the woman you mentioned yesterday, the one who knows everything about everyone?"

"You mean Fran Baker."

"How about asking her—"

"No."

"Why not?"

"Because I talked to her today about…other things and it's uncomfortable. I just don't want her to get any more involved in my life."

"Your life? Hannah, we're talking the lives of a lot of other people, too."

"They're dead, Jack. David is dead. You'll find out who else is involved and bring them to justice, but meanwhile, I've got some pretty big problems of my own to contend with. Aubrielle has to come first."

"What about the practice sessions I saw—"

"That more innocent lives are in danger is your supposition. For all we know they practice things like that 'til the cows come home just in case."

He narrowed his eyes. "What happened with this woman today?"

She looked down at her hands. How did everything get so complicated?

"Hannah? Please?"

"She informed me there's a rumor going around the foundation that I was seeing David, then she asked me point-blank if David was Aubrielle's father and I told her no."

"Are you sure you should lie to her?"

"I'm not sure of anything anymore," Hannah said, and though that was true, she was painfully aware that Jack's belief David was Aubrielle's father was the real lie.

"Listen, Hannah, if she's a know-it-all, that's exactly why you should ask her some pointed questions."

"You told me earlier to play it safe."

"Safe isn't working." He ran a hand through his hair. "I can't just sit here day after day waiting."

"I'm not asking you to sit here day after day," she said. "That was your idea."

"Yeah, well, maybe it was a stupid idea."

"Maybe it was. In fact, I'm sure it was. You should be outside this house, investigating things. It's been a couple of days now and nothing more has happened to me or my family, so maybe it was all some kind of giant, I don't know, mistake."

"Wait a second. Are you suggesting someone *mistakenly* threw a rock through your window with a note tied to it? Was it meant for someone else whose car happened to get blown up that day?"

She glared at him. The silence between them stretched

like a taut thread until the phone on the desk rang. It sounded like a fire alarm in the quiet room. She grabbed it before it could wake Aubrielle. "Yes?"

"It's me," a female voice said.

Hannah turned her back on Jack's glowering face. "Fran? What's up?"

"Mr. Correa has some papers he wants you to sign so they can get into tonight's mail. Something to do with the open house—what else?"

"He wants me to drive back into work? Now?"

"No, I'll deliver them. I'm going to a friend's house a few miles north of you so I'll be coming right through Allota in about fifteen minutes. I know it's short notice, but my cell lost its signal until I got up to the top of the bluff. I could come to your place but it might be easier if you meet me at the car park on the beach."

"Sure, I could do that."

"I don't remember how big and crowded it is. Shall we say the north end in fifteen minutes?"

"You got it."

She hung up and faced Jack. "I have to meet someone at the beach."

"Fran?"

"How did you know—"

"You said her name. This is great. It's the perfect opportunity for you to ask her about who else traveled to Tierra Montañosa the April before this one."

He never gave up. Well, she didn't, either. "I'll see," she said.

"Damn it, Hannah—"

"Don't swear at me," she warned him.

He ground his teeth, took a deep breath and nodded. "Okay, sorry. But you're going to have—"

"I don't have to do anything, Jack." She moved to

the door, stopped and turned. "Since this situation is hardly working out the way you want, why don't you pack up your stuff while I'm gone? Maybe that man will even trade you back your Harley for the truck. Cut your losses here, go after the people you're so sure are up to something horrible. Just leave me out of it."

"Knowing that David traveled to South America and lied about it and brought back all that money, you can still pretend—"

"You take care of that, I'll take care of my family, okay? We don't have to be enemies, it's just time for you to go, that's all. Grandma will listen for Aubrielle while I'm gone. You're officially off the job."

"Why do I always get the feeling there's something else going on with you?" he asked with a suspicious glint in his eyes. "At first I thought you were trying to protect someone, and I was right, you were. David. Then when there were still barriers, I attributed it to the sexual thing between us. And I was right about that, too."

"Honestly—"

"But it's obvious there's something else."

"This is your imagination talking, you know that, don't you?"

"Are you sure, *cariño?*" he murmured, stepping closer. "Do you really believe that?" He wrapped his fingers around her arms and stared into her eyes. It was like trying to absorb the blazing fury of a flamethrower.

But worse—she burned with the desire to tell him the truth about their baby, to trust him.

"I don't have time for this," she whispered, and, gently pulling free, walked out of the room. She knew he stared after her; his gaze burned holes in the back of her head.

After ducking into the kitchen for a quick word with

her grandmother, she grabbed her purse and her grandmother's car keys and left the house, refusing to think
about the wisdom of what she'd just done, refusing to
consider the risk she was taking, refusing to question
the sinking feeling in her heart. There would be time
for that later.

The beach car park was surprisingly full for a late
weekday afternoon, both with commuters carpooling
and with visitors to the rocky shoreline. On the bluff
above the beach, a collection of steeplelike rocks gave
the impression of a castle. Hannah had played there as
a kid when she stayed with her grandparents, usually
after her mother hooked up with one husband or the
other. She cast it a fond look now.

Five minutes later it became obvious Fran had mis-
judged how long it would take her to drive the last few
miles. Hannah got out of the car and looked around.
Most of the vehicles appeared empty but there were a
couple of vans without windows and work logos on their
doors along with several cars in which people waited
for one reason or another.

And all of a sudden, she felt watched...

There were concrete restrooms a few hundred feet
away. No one occupied the sidewalks in front of them.
Just to make sure, she circled the buildings, even darting
inside the women's. She couldn't quite bring herself to
peek in the men's....

She turned and scanned the beach. It was covered
with jagged dark rocks. A whole SWAT team could
be tucked out of sight behind those boulders and she
wouldn't know it.

It was with a tremendous sigh of relief that she recognized Fran's car rolling through the gates.

IF SOMEONE HAD POINTED A GUN AT his head and demanded to know why he stopped in the nursery to take one last look at Hannah's baby, Jack could not have explained himself. He stood next to Aubrielle's crib for a few seconds, some of his anger abating as he watched the tiny girl sleep.

Carefully, he lowered his hand until one large brown finger brushed her pink cheek. "Bye, Abby," he whispered. "See you around."

Now he had to face Aubrielle's great-grandmother whom he suspected might be annoyed he had agreed to abandon them.

A few minutes later he was driving out of Allota toward Fort Bragg, Mimi's teary eyes something he wasn't proud of. Well, she would have to take up her tears with her granddaughter, not with him. Not his fault.

Still, he hoped Hannah knew what she was doing by asking—okay, telling—him to leave. But maybe she was right, maybe spinning his wheels at her house was a giant waste of time.

Face it, wasn't there the tiniest bit of him that was relieved to be free again? He'd had months of imprisonment, of being told what to do and when to do it. Wasn't it great to be on the road, to have control again? If Hannah Marks wanted to put blinders on and limit her concern to just her family, who was he to stand in her way? He had bigger fish to fry.

Maybe Hannah's reluctance to face the violence that was slowly seeping around the edges of her controlled life was that she was afraid of what she'd find. Maybe she'd been afraid for so long she'd gotten used to it.

So, Jack, think. David, a man Jack knew from experience could be bought, had traveled secretly to Ecuador a few weeks before the ambush. He'd come home with a huge hunk of money he'd given to someone to hold overnight until he could go to a bank. He got called into work before he could retrieve the money. On his way to this impromptu job, he was killed in an accident.

Soon after that, Hannah's apartment was broken into and the other mishaps she'd alluded to had started. It seemed to have come to a head just recently with direct threats at her family's safety and directions to stop what she was doing. She claimed she was doing nothing.

Was she lying? There was something not quite right. Did she know more than she was willing to tell him?

Yes, he was sure of it.

What about the upcoming open house and the governor showing up? Could David's money be totally unconnected? Could this have something to do with California politics?

No way to know for sure.

Okay, first thing: find out about David's accident. Get the name of the guy who ran him over and check on him. Maybe go out to the foundation and do a little snooping, think of a disguise...

Use your head. *Hurry.*

HANNAH HAD KNOWN HER HOURS would increase as the foundation's anniversary celebration grew closer, but when a call came the very next morning to come into work for an emergency, she wished she had the option of saying no.

Things were just so unsettled. Mimi was anxious and looked as though she hadn't slept, Aubrielle was fussier than normal and Hannah's head ached. However, Harrison Plumber made it very clear he wanted her to personally straighten out a mix-up with the caterers and as all the contact information was at the office, there was no choice.

Mimi once again invited her poker ladies to come babysit with her and promised this time she wouldn't send anyone home before Hannah returned. As soon as the ladies started trickling in, Hannah kissed her sweet infant goodbye and left, driving the road to Fort Bragg distracted by her concerns for her family and her sadness over the way things had ended with Jack.

She liked him. He was a little on the intense side and not the kind a woman should ever count on to be around for several decades, but there was something inherently likeable about him that went beyond basic sex appeal. Watching him interact with her daughter was gut-wrenching on one hand, but it touched her to witness small acts of fondness on his part.

Better he was gone. Better for him, better for Aubrielle, better for Hannah.

By the time she parked at the foundation, her headache had gone from barely there to splitting and she began to think longingly of the aspirin bottle in her desk drawer. As she pushed open the lobby door, she ran into Hugo Correa, who was coming out.

Hugo closely resembled his father in looks. Both men were solid, stately, both had deep brown eyes and round faces. Where Santi's hair had grown completely white, however, Hugo's was salt-and-pepper and he wore it shorter than his father. He was also a snappier dresser, preferring well-fitted suits to the casual clothes his father wore.

Since his capture, he'd developed a limp due to the injury suffered when the GTM had shot him in the leg. It wasn't always obvious; sometimes it was much worse than other times. Today it was barely noticeable.

"Mr. Correa," she said with a pleasant smile. "How are you—"

He cast her a look that not only stole the words from her mouth but sent a visceral jolt to the middle of her stomach. Her hand unconsciously flew up to her throat. Breaking eye contact, he kept walking without saying even a word.

She turned in the door to look after him, confused at the lingering sense of unease the encounter had created.

And then it came to her—the rumor about her and David. He must have heard it. With fingers pressed to her forehead, she passed into the inner hallway and almost made it past Fran's door before Fran called out.

"Hannah? What's wrong?"

"Nothing," Hannah said, pausing. There was a man perched on the edge of Fran's desk, his back to Hannah. He wore a black suit, his black hair cut short.

"Are you sure?" Fran asked.

"Just a headache," Hannah responded, staring at the man's back.

"You just didn't seem yourself last night at the car park," Fran continued.

Really, did she have to discuss things like this with a stranger listening in? Okay, so she'd been odd. Upset about Jack and still fidgety over that feeling of being watched, she'd been more than happy to sign the stupid papers and go home, letting Fran deal with mailing them. She hadn't been her usual efficient self.

"Do you need something for your head?" Fran pressed. "I have—"

"No, I have aspirin in my desk. Thanks anyway."

"Hey, before you escape," Fran added, "let me introduce you to Jack Carlin. Jack, this is Hannah Marks."

The man turned and smiled at her. She'd known whom to expect from the phony ID name, but seeing him eye to eye, up close and personal, sitting on Fran's desk as though he belonged there still took a little getting used to.

"Pleased to meet you," Jack said, smiling.

"I met Jack last night," Fran gushed. "He was waiting out front for me when I got home."

Jack got to his feet and extended a hand. Hannah shook it and he passed her a blue business card. "Carlin Real Estate" was printed in bold black letters. Obviously, he'd discovered the quickie business card dispenser at the mall.

"Pleased to meet you," Jack said. He looked so different with his hair cut, more like he had a year before, more civilized, less risky if you discounted the reckless look in his eyes. "I'm new to Fort Bragg," he continued. "I was driving around last night looking at what's available and I ran across the sign on Ms. Baker's front lawn. What a great location she has. I hung around to talk to her about it in case her current broker can't move the property."

Hannah was about to ask if that was an ethical thing for a real estate broker to do when she came to her senses and went along with it.

"I didn't know you were selling your house," Hannah said.

Fran shrugged her slim shoulders. "I want something a little roomier. Anyway, Jack and I had fun talking about land values and such. I'm going to help him get acquainted."

Jack beamed at her. "Fran promised me a tour of the foundation. It's quite a set-up you have here."

Fran cast him a flirty look that included a wink.

Whoa. Had Jack worked a little night-time Costa del Rio magic on Fran? Hannah's head was two seconds away from exploding.

"Are you a home owner?" Jack asked. He was speaking to her.

"Uh—no. I live with my grandmother."

He managed to look disappointed. "Ah," he said.

"Well, it was nice to meet you, Mr. Carlin."

"The pleasure is all mine. If your grandmother ever decides to sell her house, I hope you'll encourage her to give me a call."

With a glimpse over her shoulder as she exited, Hannah saw him resettle on Fran's desk.

Three aspirin and two hours later, Hannah had cleared up the catering issue if not the headache. She had purposely closed her door in order to concentrate without the distractions of seeing Jack and Fran. The thought he'd taken her to bed last night ate away at her although she had no right to care one way or another.

More pressing, or at least it should be, was what to do about Hugo Correa's obvious unhappiness with her. In all the years she'd known him, he'd never been anything but polite and generous. This morning's cold shoulder was disquieting. How did she fix it?

If she could take back the months with David she would in a heartbeat. Maybe she should have come forward after his death and admitted their affair, but it had seemed too little too late by then and really, in so many ways, their relationship had not seemed like that big a deal.

All justification. She'd screwed up everything lately and no doubt as soon as the open house was over, she'd be asked to look for work elsewhere. Play the game, pay the price.

She looked around for Harrison Plumber to assure him everything was ironed out and found he'd left for the day, so she sent him an e-mail. Fran wasn't in her office when Hannah made her way out of the lobby. Jack must be getting the deluxe tour....

It was sunny outside although she could glimpse a fog bank hovering over the hills toward the ocean. Great. It would be cold and dismal in Allota. There went her planned beach walk with Aubrielle.

She was only a few feet from the building when Jack dislodged himself from the old truck he'd traded his bike for and approached. He'd obviously been waiting for her.

"I'd like to talk to you about your grandmother's property," he said in a loud voice although Hannah couldn't see anyone else around.

"It's not for sale, Mr. Carlin," she said in an equally carrying tone.

"Everything is for sale, Ms. Marks," he said.

"Including Fran Baker?" she asked, voice much lower now.

He smiled. "Actually, I have something to tell you about your friend Fran and I'm not sure how you're going to take it."

"Let me guess. She's an undercover terrorist with the GTM?"

"Funny."

"I thought you were nervous about Hugo or Harrison recognizing you."

"I was. I am. But I figured it was time to take a few chances. Stop stalling. You need to know Fran broke the same company policy you broke at about the same time you were breaking it."

"She dated someone from Staar?"

He nodded.

She didn't want to talk about this. "Why didn't you get your Harley back?" she asked.

"I like the truck."

"Sure you do."

"I'm evolved, remember? Don't you want to know who Fran was seeing?"

"No. I'm tired of gossip. I can't believe she actually told you such a thing. Pillow talk?"

"Damn it," he said, stopping suddenly and grabbing her wrists. "Knock it off, Hannah."

She closed her eyes. "Okay. Sorry."

"No, it wasn't pillow talk, it was Fran talk." He shoved his hands into his pockets. "The woman rarely shuts up. I know it's going to hurt you but it's better you find out from me." He took a deep breath. "She was seeing David."

"*My* David?"

"Your David. He was two-timing you."

She ran her fingers over her face, messaging her temples for a moment. She should be furious, right? Livid at David, maybe at Fran, too. The fact was she felt very little of anything. Fran could have had David lock, stock and barrel if he'd survived.

Was this why Fran had been so curious about Aubrielle's paternity? If she'd loved David, knowing another woman had his child would have hurt.

"That's not all," Jack said.

There was more? "Okay," she said, resuming walking. More then ever she wanted to get home. He bypassed his truck to stay with her. "Fran said a lot of people from the foundation went to Ecuador before the ambush on a semirelated trip. Some funding issue. Santi, Hugo, Harrison Plumber, some guy named Jenkins."

"They went to Ecuador at the same time as David? Did Fran mention that?"

"No. Who's Jenkins?"

"He's the CPA. How could I have not remembered they went? There was just so much going on at the time. My grandfather's illness, my mother's fourth marriage, David and me falling apart—"

"As long as we're comparing notes," Jack interrupted, "I went out to see the guy who killed David."

"The trucker?"

"Mitch Reynolds. He and his family live in a pretty ratty part of town, out over the bridge past an old rock quarry. His house looks like a asthmatic wolf could blow it over."

"So?"

"So, there's a very large, very expensive red SUV parked in his driveway and before you say he had a visitor, I checked the registration."

"He probably owes a fortune on the thing."

"No. He bought it with cash. The guys at the dealership are still talking about it. There's a new RV parked by the side of the garage, too. And get this, one of the guys at the dealership mentioned that Reynolds occasionally worked out at Staar."

"A lot of people work here once in a while."

"No doubt. But it connects him."

This man's talents were obviously wasted guarding a baby. "On the other hand, what does a new car this year have to do with David's death a year ago?"

"He bought it two weeks after David died. It made a big impression on the salesman. He'd read about the accident in the newspaper."

"What exactly are you saying?"

"I'm saying it looks as though Reynolds may have

been paid to run into David. I'll have to figure out a way to talk to him, see if he was on his regular route. We already know he worked on and off again at Staar."

"I don't know, Jack."

"The call that morning to David might have been a setup," he continued. "If he and a partner arranged the ambush and then if David took all the GTM money and the partner wanted it back or wanted to shut David's mouth, it could explain everything."

"Except someone warning me to knock off what I'm doing—'or else,'" she said.

"Yeah."

She'd stopped moving to listen. Walking again, she said, "People get windfalls. A relative dies, whatever. Maybe the trucker just spent his on toys."

She stopped talking when she got a glimpse of her grandmother's car. It twinkled in the sunlight as though paved with diamonds. "The windshield!" she cried as the cell phone in her handbag rang. She grabbed it by habit, still gaping at the car. Jack stepped past her to survey the damage.

"Hannah, it's me, Grandma," Mimi said.

"Grandma. You aren't going to believe what's happened now." A silent pause cut through Hannah's distress. "Grandma? Grandma, what is it?"

Mimi's voice caught as she whispered, "Come home quickly. Aubrielle is gone."

Chapter Nine

"What do you mean, *gone?*" Jack demanded as Hannah slid into the truck next to him. He was in gear and taking off up the hill before her door was completely closed.

She sat staring straight ahead, her arms wrapped around each other. He could feel her body trembling. They were twenty minutes away form Allota and that was driving with all the stops out. "Hannah? Tell me what your grandmother said."

She turned stricken eyes at him. "I could barely understand her. Something about a fire."

"What did she say when you told her to call the police?"

"She said the note said 'No cops.'"

"But she still has to call them," he argued.

Hannah shook her head. "She refused. She said I would understand, just to hurry."

"You call them," he said.

Again she shook her head. "No."

"But—"

"Grandma said the note implied this was a warning, Aubrielle would survive only if the police weren't called. Drive faster."

He drove faster, halfway hoping some alert highway patrolman would chase him down so he could enlist aid. His mind raced—the obvious: he shouldn't have let Hannah fire him. He'd left the child in danger—why had he allowed that?

He slid a look at his frantic passenger. He knew she was beating herself up for leaving the baby with her grandmother and friends. No doubt her grandmother was sick that the baby had been taken on her watch.

But the bottom line was if amoral jerks wanted to wreak havoc on normal people, it was damn near impossible to stop them. Hadn't that been the final lesson of the ambush in Tierra Montañosa? Didn't every suicide bomber reinforce that one fact?

"It's so foggy and cold," Hannah whispered as they sped down the hill toward Allota.

"We're almost there." Those were the last words either of them spoke until they pulled onto Mimi's street. A fire truck was parked close by, its crew coiling up hoses, and for a second, Jack felt like scratching his newly shorn head, trying to figure out where a fire truck fit into this debacle. Then Hannah pointed at what was left of the old abandoned car across from Mimi's house. Reduced to a smoldering black frame, acrid smoke still hung in the air around it.

Mimi and two other women erupted out of Mimi's house as Jack pulled into the driveway. Hannah had her door open and had jumped out before he could fully stop the truck. By the time he stepped inside the house, just the two friends were visible. They met his gaze and nodded anxiously toward the hall.

He kept going, heart pounding, pausing at the doorway to the nursery. Hannah and Mimi were standing inside the room, Hannah comforting Mimi as her stricken eyes searched the empty room for her child. A pain shot right through the middle of his chest.

Though now filled with three adults, the fact the baby who belonged here was missing made the place feel abandoned. Hannah met his gaze, her eyes swimming in tears that rolled down her cheeks when she blinked. She held out a piece of white paper. He made his way around her in order to peer over her shoulder at the note, which was written in a weird loopy font most computer printers could produce.

"This is a last warning," it read. *"Any further attempts to blackmail me will result in immediate and irrevocable measures taken against your baby. You are being watched. Do not contact the police. Use your head (what was good for you is good for me) and you'll know where she is—this time. One hint of police involvement and you'll never see your baby again."*

"What does this mean?" Hannah cried. "Blackmail? I'm not blackmailing anyone."

"We'll think about that later," Jack said, driven by nerves to pace the small pink room. The empty crib and open window were like pointing fingers.

"I shouldn't have fired you," Hannah said, meeting his gaze over her sobbing grandmother's head.

He looked at her tear-streaked face and shook his head. "I shouldn't have left." He took a deep breath. Going to Mimi, he took her hands and led her to the rocking chair where she sat down heavily. "Quick now, Mimi, tell us exactly what happened."

Mimi's hands fluttered helplessly on her lap as she spoke. "The girls and I were in the living room," she began. "Aubrielle had just taken the milk Hannah left for her and had gone to sleep, so I put her in her crib. Then Barb noticed a commotion outside, and we realized the old wreck across the street was on fire."

"Did you see anyone hanging around?"

"No. No one. Barb called the fire department and they were here within minutes and we watched as they arrived to put out the fire and then I got a feeling I should check on Aubrielle and she was…she was… gone." At this point, Mimi's tears started anew. She wiped at her papery cheeks with a tissue. "I shouldn't have allowed myself to become distracted. I should have kept her right in my arms."

"It's not your fault," Hannah and Jack said in unison.

She shook her head.

"Hannah, think," Jack said. "The comment the kidnapper made about you knowing where Aubrielle is, that the place was good enough for you so it's good enough for them. Does that mean anything to you?"

"No," she said, her hands clenched at her sides. "I'm not blackmailing anyone. How can that make sense?"

"Look at it from the point of view of whoever is doing this. We're going to have to make some leaps here and if we can't come up with something very quickly, we're going to have to call the cops. Let's think of the main people who keep coming into the picture."

"What do you mean?" she cried and he could see nerves and fear clouding her head.

"Think, honey," he said firmly and softly. "People like Fran, for instance."

"But Fran was with you this morning."

"When did this happen?" he asked Mimi.

She shook her head. One of the friends said, "Sometime in the last hour," from the doorway.

"Fran left Staar well over an hour ago," Jack said. "She said she had an appointment."

The woman at the door said, "If you don't need Mimi,

let me and Barb take her into the kitchen and make her something warm to drink."

Hannah hugged her grandmother again and they both watched the older woman leave. "I've been so incredibly selfish putting her in the middle of my mess," Hannah said. "We have to get Aubrielle back safe or Grandma will never forgive herself."

He nodded. He knew Hannah would never forgive herself, either, and frankly, neither would he forgive himself.

"Why would Fran do all this?" Hannah said. "Why would she think I would blackmail her?"

"We'll leave the why for later. Opportunity, yes. How about Hugo Correa? Fran mentioned he wasn't in today."

"He was leaving when I arrived," she said quickly. They were both talking fast, words spilling out.

"And Harrison Plumber?"

"By the time I left he was already gone. I don't know when he left."

"Who else?"

"I can't think of anyone else. It's impossible to think any of these people would—"

"Think," he interrupted her, a sense of pressing urgency building in his chest. He kept feeling the way Abby had nestled against him when he walked around town the day before, kept seeing her eyes focusing on his lips when he spoke to her. She was so tiny and so innocent. "Think of each of these people and something you might have shared with them recently. Something you planned or organized. Don't try to relate it to this."

"Like what?" she cried.

He threw up his hands. "A restaurant. A movie theatre you suggested. A—a store..."

Her gaze on the carpet, she struggled for a few seconds, then blurted out, "I volunteered to pick up dry cleaning for Harrison Plumber a few mornings ago. He was running late to catch a flight and it was on my way. Things like that?"

"Okay, what else. How about you and Fran?"

"She's the one who suggested I meet her at the beach car park yesterday but that was only because Hugo had papers he needed signed. Other than that, outside of work, I can't think of anything. Wait, I arranged flowers for a reception a few weeks ago. I used an old friend's shop and Fran complimented me on my choice."

"Okay, good. We have a dry cleaner and a florist and the car park. That leaves Hugo Correa."

With the mention of the Correa name, her gaze darted away. "I can't think of anything," she said.

He was familiar enough with her expressions that he knew something else was troubling her. "Out with it. Hurry."

"It's nothing. He just acted odd this morning. I think he knows about me and David, that he heard the stupid rumor and that he's angry. It doesn't matter, none of this matters. We have to do something. We're wasting time."

"Maybe he was mad at something else," Jack said, but he agreed with her, they had to act. Going off without a plan seemed like a bad idea.

"The thought of her alone, maybe outside—"

"That's it, of course, that's where we start, at the most dangerous place, the beach. If she's inside, she'll be safe, but outside in this cold fog…"

His voice trailed off as Hannah twirled on her heels and took off down the hall, her footsteps pounding the floor as she ran. By the time he caught up with her, she was on her way out the front door, yelling assurances at her grandmother, who watched the departure from the kitchen doorway.

He moved close to Mimi. "I need a blanket and binoculars." As she opened the closet and produced both, he added, "Mimi, there's an outside chance whoever took Aubrielle is waiting for us to leave and get far away from the house and then return her, probably by leaving her at the front door. If that happens, don't try to catch this person or even figure out who they are, just get the baby back and call Hannah, okay?"

Eyes huge, the older woman nodded.

Twenty seconds later, he stuffed the blanket and binoculars behind the seat with the shotgun he'd taken from Hannah's grandfather's gun case and climbed into the truck. Hannah cast him a look that broke his heart. Her occasional catches of breath fueled his anger. Pushing that deep inside, he concentrated on one thing: finding Aubrielle.

Later, when it was over, that's when someone would pay.

HANNAH SAW LINDY'S FLORIST as they came to the end of Main Street. In Hannah's mind, the three places they'd discussed loomed like dots on a map leading ever farther away from Allota. The florist shop in town, the beach south of town, the long stretch of oceanfront road and finally the dry cleaners in North Fort Bragg. It would waste time to bypass one in favor of another and then to have to loop back.

And if the baby was at none of these spots, what then? Risk the police?

"I'll be right back," Hannah said when Jack stopped

for a red light. She climbed out of the truck, leaving him gaping after her.

The woman who ran the shop had gone to school with Hannah's mother. Her oldest daughter, Jill, and Hannah were friends. As soon as Lindy saw Hannah race through the door, a smile of greeting creased her face.

"Hannah, I just got a postcard from your mom. Imagine her soaking up the Mediterranean sunshine while we're stuck in this dreary—"

"Have you seen her?" Hannah gasped.

"Your mother? Not since her wedding—"

"No, not my mother. My daughter. Aubrielle. Did anyone leave her with you?"

"Of course not," Lindy said, brow wrinkling. "Why would—"

That's all Hannah heard. She found Jack parked across the street, waiting. Dodging midday congestion, she darted across the road and slid into the truck.

"Nothing?" he asked as he pulled back into the stream of traffic.

"No. Go to the beach car park."

The few minutes it took to travel that far stretched out like a mini-eternity. Jack slowed down to enter through the gate and Hannah's heart continued to sink.

This close to the ocean, the fog was sitting damn near on the ground despite the brisk wind. "Go to the north end," she directed and he pulled up close to where she'd parked twenty-four hours before.

But unlike the day before, nothing was in clear-cut sight today. The Dumpster was a hulking green shape off to the left, the cinder-block bathrooms to the right a set of dull gray rectangles. Even the parked cars loomed like ghosts and the mist-draped rocks rose like the gun-metal claws of an encroaching monster.

By unspoken agreement, they both moved toward the county Dumpster, as though needing to investigate the worst thing first. Hannah's heart thumped against her ribs as she caught a whiff of rank odor. The thought someone would leave a three-month-old baby in such a contraption made her queasy. On the other hand, it would be relatively warm out of the fog-swirled wind…

Jack stepped in front of her and lifted the lid. She could tell he was trying to protect her but the truth was there was no way to shield her if her baby was in this Dumpster. No comforting words, no consolation. Aubrielle was her flesh and blood—

His flesh and blood, too…

The thought flashed into her head and she chased it away. In the next instant, she held on to the edge of the metal container and peered inside.

There was nothing in it but a few random fast-food containers and the contents of an ashtray or two. Jack closed the lid with a loud bang and they both took a steadying breath.

"The restrooms," he said.

They walked quickly along the sidewalk, ducking into the respective bathrooms. Hannah opened every stall door with an increasing sense of loss. After the Dumpster proved fruitless, she'd been sure she'd find Aubrielle inside this building because, face it, where else did you leave a very small child at such a desolate spot? If she wasn't here, she was outside and that thought was untenable.

Wait—the dry cleaner. She'd forgotten the dry cleaner. "Hannah?" Jack shouted from outside.

Hannah realized she'd been standing, staring into the

last empty stall with tears running down her cheeks. At the sound of his voice, she turned and left the building. Maybe Jack had found her!

He shook his head in defeat as his gaze took in her equally empty arms. That left the vast, dangerous, cold beach.

Squealing brakes behind them announced the arrival of a car. It parked a few feet away. The male driver sat there a second, his red hair so vibrant it was like a drop of blood in the gray and white world. Hannah's heart was on the verge of implosion.

At last the door opened and a wiry guy wearing a white hooded sweatshirt with a large black and gold *fleur de lis* on the chest stepped out.

Jack moved in front of Hannah. She could feel the coiled tension in his body.

"Awful day for the beach," the man grumbled, and, giving them a wide berth, disappeared into the men's room.

As the door closed behind him, both Jack and Hannah raced to the car and peered in every window. Between its size and design, there were no hiding spots. A briefcase, a wooden dowel half buried under a raincoat, a fedora—nothing else, most important, *no baby*.

They stepped back onto the sidewalk just as the driver reappeared, his hands stuffed into the long single pocket that ran across the front of his hoodie.

Hannah couldn't take her eyes from him, but he ignored her and made straight for his car. In another few seconds, he'd driven away.

"He was nobody," Hannah whispered.

"Just a traveler with a full bladder," Jack added. He turned to face the beach again. Without speaking, they both stepped onto the sand and began navigating their way around the rocks, searching the gaps and crevices for some sign of Aubrielle. It resembled a bizarre Easter egg hunt with the hope of a priceless reward.

Their search was frantic by nature, thorough by necessity. Eventually, they ended up near the slack tide, the ocean strangely quiet as the waves lapped the beach, as if it, too, held its breath.

"It's impossible," Jack said, staring out at what was visible of the water. "I should go back to the truck for the binoculars."

"We should have called the dry cleaner," she said, fumbling with her phone, but in her panic she couldn't even remember the name of the place.

"Call your grandmother. Make sure the baby wasn't returned to the house."

A surge of hope was crushed as Mimi explained she and her friends had searched the perimeter of the house several times for some sign of Aubrielle and come up empty. At Hannah's urging, one of the friends recalled the name of the dry cleaner and used her cell to call them to ask if someone had left a baby in their care. "They thought she was joking," Mimi reported a minute later. "Oh, Hannah, what are we going to do?"

Hannah hung up the phone. Jack's tall form had moved away from her toward the water. Dressed in his dark suit and black loafers, he made an incongruous sight on the gray deserted beach, a strong dark shape in the shifting fog.

Something about the way he stood alerted her and she moved toward him, directing her gaze out to where he looked. She'd almost reached him when she caught sight of something floating in the water. Something pinkish...

In a flash, he'd begun running through the waves,

water splashing against his legs as he plowed through them on an interception pass with whatever it was.

For the umpteenth time that day, Hannah all but stopped breathing as she followed him, stopping short when, in waist-high water, he scooped something out of the water and held it high, turning back to her so she could see. She stood there frozen by fear.

And then she realized he held a mass of seaweed with some kind of cloth running through it. Dragging it back with him, he trudged through the water, wet now from his waist down. For the first time, the numbing cold of the water registered in Hannah's brain and she shuddered from her mist-dampened hair to her frozen toes.

Jack was beside her, dropping the sodden mess on the sand. Hannah knelt to investigate. What if it was a piece of Aubrielle's blanket or clothing…?

But it wasn't. It appeared to be a man's shirt and from the way it had twisted and twined in the kelp, it had been in the water a long time.

Jack touched her shoulder and she looked up at him. "We can't just wait for this person to decide to return her," he said.

Tears that had been rolling down her cheeks and soaking into her coat for an hour erupted into a terrified sob.

He gathered her into his arms, holding her tight, pressing her against his solid chest. She allowed herself a few seconds and then she pushed herself from the haven of his arms.

"That officer you like, Latimer, right?" he said, his eyes searching hers. "Let's get him to meet us somewhere. It'll be easier talking face-to-face with him than trying to explain all this over the phone."

*You are being watched. One hint of police involve-
ment and you'll never see your baby again.*

"But what if—"

He shook his head. "I'm going to be blunt. Abby is
too tiny to survive outdoors. We don't have a choice, we
need help before it's too late," he said.

She drew strength from the conviction in his voice.
She knew he was right. "Okay."

"Let's go back to the house and call him from that
phone just in case. Think of a good spot to meet him.
We'll think of a diversion of some kind."

His voice trailed off. Was he thinking someone could
tap her cell phone? He took her hand and kept it in his
all the way back across the beach. The car park had
an isolated, forsaken feel to it. The whole world felt
forsaken. Jack opened her door and moved aside.

For a second she stared at the crumpled green sweater
on the front seat. She didn't remember it being there
before, but maybe Jack had grabbed it from the house
before they left in hopes they'd soon need it to wrap
around Aubrielle. It was her grandmother's favorite, the
one with the orange and brown trim, the huge one that
was more coat than sweater.

There was something pinned to it, another note,
printed out like the last one, upside down to Hannah
although she could make out the first line: *Next time
the old lady.*

As fury and frustration collided in Hannah's gut, she
grabbed for the sweater and the note, almost mindless
in light of the implications of yet another unfathomable
threat.

At the last minute, Jack reached around her and
grabbed her wrist. "No, Hannah," he said.

Had he seen something? A bomb hidden in the folds? Anything seemed possible.

And then she saw it, too. Movement. The sweater was wrapped around something—

An outraged cry, a hearty kick and a tiny foot emerged from beneath the bundle. Heart leaping into her throat, Hannah quickly spread the sweater open.

Aubrielle's very pink, very outraged face came into view. Hannah swayed for a second as relief sapped the strength out of her bones. Jack steadied her. In the next instant, she'd gathered her baby into her arms, never so glad to hold anyone in her entire life.

She was hardly aware when Jack unpinned the note, glanced at it briefly and put it in his pocket.

Chapter Ten

"Get in the truck, Hannah."

Apparently hearing the urgency in his voice, she held the baby tight against her chest and did as he asked. Maybe she'd had a chance to read the whole note, maybe she knew it warned that they were still being watched and if they didn't go straight home, Mimi would be next.

He swore to himself as he backed up the truck. He wasn't sure how it had happened, but these three females were now his responsibility and would be until he found whoever was doing this and stopped them.

How did he reconcile that with the gut feeling there were a lot more people a half a world away who were also depending on him to stop screwing around and figure out what was going on?

He glanced at Hannah and wondered what she wasn't telling him. There was something, he knew there was. Everything had been happening so fast today he hadn't had a chance to think, but he could feel she was holding something back.

And since when did he go around "feeling" things? Where was his head?

Hannah was peeling away Mimi's sweater, checking out her squirming baby, making sure she was all right.

Aubrielle suffered the turning and caresses with pretty good grace although an occasional squawk seemed to him a warning Hannah better knock it off soon.

Maybe she felt him looking at her, for she looked up, flashed a smile and said, "She looks okay. Her diaper is a little soggy, but it doesn't appear whoever took her harmed her."

"That's a relief."

"Did you read the note?" she added. "May I see it? I didn't get a change to read it all."

He was glad she'd come back to earth and dug it out of his pocket and handed it to her. She read it silently as she rocked Aubrielle in her arms.

"It's time to figure out the why and the who," she said, her statement mirroring his thoughts again.

"Yes, it is," he said. "Was there anything peculiar about the money?"

"David's money? Not that I could tell. It's still in a locked box so we can go look at it tomorrow." After a moment, she added, "Fran."

"What about Fran?"

"She's the one who told me to meet her at the car park. It has to be her."

"Maybe," he said.

"How can you say, 'Maybe'?"

He rubbed his eyes. The new suit and shoes, ruined now, were sticking to him. Where he'd spent months being hot and sweaty all the time, he was now cold and clammy and needed a shower.

With her. He wanted to take Hannah into the shower with him and make love to her the way they had in Costa del Rio. He wanted hot water, soap and hot sex with *her*. No one else.

Man, he was in trouble. He needed to figure this out

and drive away from Allota and Hannah and her baby and never, ever look back.

"Jack?"

He blinked a couple of times. "The note said go to the place that was good for you."

"The car park."

"But Fran picked the car park, right? Not you. Besides, the baby wasn't waiting for us there, she arrived later, after we'd gone down to the beach, or we would have seen the whole thing. It seems to me we were followed. You could have gone anyplace. As soon as we were out of sight of the car, wham, the baby is returned along with more threats."

"But Fran knows something," Hannah persisted.

"Why do you say that?"

Hannah took a deep breath. "Gut feeling?"

He smiled. "Good. Nice to know you're thinking with something other than your head because your head has been a major stumbling—"

"What does that mean?" she interrupted.

He turned into Mimi's driveway. Before he could respond, Mimi and her friends flew out the door and it dawned on him that they hadn't called to report they had the baby. He felt ashamed of the oversight.

"What do you think of the idea of trying to get her to leave for a while?" Hannah said suddenly.

"Your grandmother? I think it's excellent. I was going to suggest something like that. Any ideas?"

"I think so. I'd rather not show her the note. It's so terrible."

"I agree."

"Jack, I also have to insist you don't contact the police. You read the note. Whoever's doing this is at least one step ahead of us and I won't risk Grandma or Aubrielle again."

"Your call," he said. If Hannah could get her grand-mother to leave, maybe he could get Hannah to take Abby and go with her.

The look on Mimi's face as Hannah climbed out of the truck carrying her baby wrapped up in Mimi's sweater was downright heartwarming. Jack shook his head at himself. He was getting soft.

Turning away from the reunion, he circled the house to the back, coming to a stop outside Aubrielle's bed-room window. His plan was to examine the softer dirt of the flower bed, hoping the foggy, damp day had softened the ground and he might be able to find a footprint.

What he found was that the kidnapper had pulled a lawn chair over to the flower bed beneath the window and used that to get high enough to gain leverage to bust the window lock.

No way was he going to call the police behind Han-nah's back, but he wasn't a cop. He didn't know how to process a crime scene or have the tools even if he had known the procedure. And then there was the fire across the street. That needed to be investigated—no way was it a coincidence.

His instinct was to bag all the notes and other in-criminating items, including the sweater, seal off the nursery and solve the crime himself. Then he could hand the criminal and the evidence to the police so they could make an arrest.

Hannah turned the corner of the house and ap-proached him. She had Abby clutched tight against her in a viselike grip.

"How's your grandmother?"

"Terrified. I asked Barb if she'd be willing to take

Grandma on a road trip, just the two of them. Barb is excited about it, Grandma is dragging her feet, but I think she'll agree."

"You and the baby could go with them," he suggested, willing her to say yes.

"No. I have to see this through. This concerns me in some way I don't understand. I'm not walking away and leaving it unfinished. This has to be someone I know. I can't hide forever."

"Then you and I and Aubrielle will go check into a hotel under my name."

She opened her mouth and he steeled himself for the protest he knew was coming. Instead, she looked over his shoulder at the violated window. He could almost feel the shudder that ran through her body as she clutched the baby even closer.

"I don't want to go back inside this house," she said softly. "I couldn't bear to put Aubrielle back in her crib or ever leave her in that nursery again. A hotel sounds great and maybe if Grandma knows we're leaving, too, she'll agree to go with Barb."

"Go convince her. Pack some things for you and the baby while you're in there. Do you want me to hold the baby?"

She gave him a once-over. "You're kind of wet," she said. "You go change and pack first, then you can relieve me and I will. Ask Grandma to come outside and I'll talk to her on the porch. I'm not taking Aubrielle inside that house again and I'm not putting her down."

She'd finally started taking everything as seriously as the situation demanded. It was a relief not to have to pry and prod her. He sent her grandmother outside, then took a quick lonely shower, changed his clothes thanks to the fact that his duffel bag was in the back of his truck, and packed what little there was left to be packed. By the time he returned to the living room, Mimi was lining two suitcases up by the door. Jack could see Hannah outside, sitting on the porch swing, Aubrielle now wrapped in a rosy blanket instead of her great-grandmother's green sweater.

"Oh, Jack, I wanted to talk to you," Mimi said. Her green sweater was looped through her arm.

He gestured at the suitcases. "You and Barb going on a drive?"

Mimi's eyes filled with moisture. "Am I doing the right thing leaving Hannah?"

"Absolutely," he assured her. "You have to leave your sweater, though. Someday the police might need it to compare fibers or something if they get a suspect. I'll put it in the closet for you."

"What about my car? Hannah said someone broke the windshield."

"I already called a garage. They're towing it in for you. Don't worry."

She nodded as he took the sweater and returned with a brown coat he'd seen her wear.

"I wouldn't go if she didn't have you to depend on," Mimi said as she took the coat.

Him to depend on. Innocent enough words, so why did they make him quake inside?

"I'll pay you, you know, whatever the going rate is for being a bodyguard."

"We'll work it out later," he told her, and surprised himself by leaning down and kissing her cheek. He was glad she'd reminded him this was a professional situation. He was the baby's bodyguard, that's all.

She patted his face. "I like your haircut though I have to admit it was sexier before."

"It'll grow back," he told her, smiling.

A big blue sedan pulled up outside. "That's Barb," Mimi said, hefting the smaller suitcase. Jack took the larger one in hand. "You take care of my girls, okay?"

With a sudden pang of fondness for Mimi, he put a hand on her shoulder. "Mimi, be sure you register under Barb's name. And share a room with her. And keep going, don't spend more than one night in any one place. If you feel threatened by anyone or anything, go to the cops. Call Hannah every night."

She laughed at him. "You make it sound like I'm on the lam," she said as they walked out onto the porch.

He helped Mimi load her things into Barb's trunk and stood silently by as Hannah and her grandmother said their goodbyes. Hannah stood on the sidewalk watching the big blue car roll down the street as he retreated to the porch and waited for her to relinquish control of her baby. He wanted to get out of there. He was way too aware someone might be watching them.

She eventually wandered back onto the porch but still she lingered. He guessed her reluctance to part with Abby had to do with maternal instincts and the terror of the afternoon, but man, get it over with. He finally more or less took the bundled baby from her hands and pushed her through the door.

"Watch her head," Hannah demanded.

"Go pack," he said.

The baby made a little crying noise as he jostled her and Hannah almost turned back. "Hannah," he said sternly. "Go pack. We'll be fine."

She finally left.

"Your mommy is a little clingy," he told Abby as he made sure he was supporting her head and not smothering her in the blanket. The baby stopped fussing at the sound of his voice, her gaze more or less glued to his face. It seemed she was waiting for something. He sat down on the swing seat and gently got it moving, holding the baby on his lap, one hand supporting the back of her neck, the other under her legs.

The melody and words of a song he'd heard down in Tierra Montañosa ran through his head. One of the women who cleaned the office had brought a small baby in to work with her sometimes and she'd sung to him as she moved around the place. Until that second, Jack didn't even know he'd picked up the lyrics. Making sure no one was watching him or listening, he looked right into Abby's eyes and tried singing.

"Duerme, niño chiquito," he crooned, wincing at the sound of his voice. There would be no music awards in his future. *"Duerme, mi alma; Duérmete lucerito, De la mañana."*

Abby didn't fall asleep, but she did continue staring at him, and for a second, he experienced one of his Zen moments, one of those rod-through-the-head, out-the-feet, right-on-through-to-the-center-of-the-earth moments and he hadn't even tried to get there.

"The power of music, huh, Abby?" he said, and damn if it didn't look to him like she smiled.

Hannah practically burst through the door looking more harried than she had when she left the porch. Her arms were full of baby stuff and a diaper bag was slung over one shoulder. She looked at the two of them with anxious eyes.

"It's okay, she's fine," he assured her.

"THE SAME ROOM?" SHE SAID when he came back to the truck with a single key.

"The same room," he insisted. "I'm Abby's bodyguard, remember? That means I need her close by and you come as part of the package."

She narrowed her eyes. "Her name is Aubrielle."

"I know her name," he said.

His tone suggested he would call the baby what he wanted to. It seemed stupid to argue about it because she knew the only reason she cared was because she was feeling territorial. When she'd glanced out the window an hour before and witnessed him singing a Spanish lullaby to *her* enraptured infant, she'd freaked out.

"Okay, okay," she said.

He started the truck and drove into an underground parking garage. He'd insisted they stay in a place with no exterior door leading to their room and now he informed her they were on the fourth floor so there'd be no surprises through the windows.

"What did you mean when you said you were glad I was thinking with my gut?" she asked.

He cast her a quick look, then pulled the truck into an opening close to the elevator. "Because whatever you're still hiding from me has had you more scared than the very real threats of a person willing to enter your house in the daylight, twice, and the second time take your child. That's finally changed and that's because this person finally hit you hard enough to get your gut working. I, for one, am grateful."

She shook her head.

As they packed everything into the elevator and rode up to their floor, she asked him what his plans were.

"I'm going to go see Fran."

"Why? Do you have a buyer for her house?"

He smiled down at her. "You sound jealous, *cariño*."

"Ha."

"After you kicked me out yesterday, I looked her up. When I saw the For Sale sign, I drove back to what passes for a mall around here, bought a suit, got a haircut and made up some business cards. When she returned, I flattered and flirted my way into her house. I lied to her. I ate her food, which was at least not burned, and I laughed at her jokes. I heard about everyone she works with, especially you and David. I think she started the supposed 'rumor.' I wouldn't be surprised if she knows he was Abby's father."

Hannah made a fuss over shifting Aubrielle's slumbering body in her arms so she wouldn't be expected to respond.

"Anyway, tonight I'll confess all my sins. Women appreciate groveling. Maybe she'll talk some more."

"You said the car park location didn't necessarily lead things back to her."

"I know. But I'd bet a few bucks she knows more than she's telling. Like that trip she mentioned those four men taking. What was that about? It would have been a perfect opportunity for David to meet with one of them or more and if she was intimate with David, sorry for mentioning that, maybe she knows who. And if we have a *who* I can get him to open up, so to say, to spill his guts and reveal what's going on with you and the Staar Foundation—"

"You're getting ahead of yourself," she said softly.

"I feel as though I'm stuck in quicksand," he said.

"Aubrielle and I will go to Fran's house with you."

"No, you won't. I'll ask hotel security to keep an eye on the room. You and Abby stay put."

"You can't help yourself, can you? Stop bossing me around. Fran is my friend, I'm going. If she knows something about what's happening to me, she's more likely to tell me than you, especially when she figures out you lied to her about being a real estate agent."

"You're the most stubborn woman I've ever met," he said as he unlocked the door.

The room contained a table and chair in a corner, a dresser and TV and two queen-sized beds that seemed to stretch from wall to wall. They piled all their things on the bed closest to the door. Hannah pulled back the bedspread—everyone knew how seldom they were laundered—and laid the baby on the clean white sheets. When she looked up, Jack was staring at her, his expression so intense she got the feeling the memories of their one night together in a hotel room were running as vividly through his mind as they were hers.

He put a hand on the bed and pushed gently as though testing the softness of the mattress. The sight of his tan fingers pressing against the crisp white cotton sent a quiver through her core and for a second she was tempted, she was very tempted....

"Let's go see Fran," she said.

FRAN LIVED ON A CUL-DE-SAC AT the end of a street where half the houses were either empty, for sale or both. Hannah had been there a few times in the past for a party or to give rides when Fran's car broke down.

The garage was wide open and her car—a new one, the old wreck had disappeared several months before— was parked inside so at least she was home. They hadn't called first figuring surprise might be best.

Aubrielle was still asleep. This time Hannah loosened the car seat from its anchors and carried it with her to the front door. Jack offered to take it from her but she declined. Yes, it was bulky and heavy but the less Jack did with Aubrielle, the better.

Jack rang the bell and knocked. Then he tried the knob.

"It's locked," he said as it refused to twist.

"Since she left work so early, maybe she's working on her garden," Hannah volunteered.

"In this weather?" Jack said as he zipped his leather jacket. "She told me she was leaving for an appointment. She didn't say anything about gardening."

"You have a better idea?"

They moved around the south side of the house and through the gate. There was no sign of Fran or any indication she'd done any gardening that day. A peek through the sliding glass door revealed an orderly dining room and kitchen. Jack tried that door as well and she wondered if he planned on entering the house. "Locked," he said.

Back in front, they passed the open garage. Maybe Fran had exited through the garage door to take a walk, but it seemed odd not to lock up behind her with the neighborhood so empty and the garage filled with tempting things. Plus the weather was still drippy and gray.

"There's a door into the house at the back of the garage," Jack said peering inside.

"It enters into her laundry room," Hannah murmured.

He stepped into the heavy shadows of the garage and Hannah followed. She'd gone no farther than Fran's rear bumper when the hairs rose on the back of her neck. She couldn't see anything amiss, but on some sensory level, she *felt* something was wrong.

"Jack, I have a feeling—"

He put a hand back and touched her chest. "Stay there, please," he said, his voice soft.

He was standing opposite the driver's window and

now he stepped closer and peered inside. His body jerked backward in an involuntary startle. In that instant, Hannah knew he'd found Fran.

With a warning look at her, he approached the back door. He unzipped his jacket and, using it to shield his hand, tried her knob. The door didn't budge.

Jack returned to Hannah with a resolute look on his face, his mouth a grim line.

"What happened to Fran?" Hannah whispered.

"She's dead."

"How?"

The baby carrier was suddenly in his hands instead of hers and she realized she'd been on the verge of dropping it. He put another hand on her arm and propelled her away. "Someone shot her in the face," he said softly.

Hannah sagged a little more.

"Call the police," he added.

She took out her cell, anxiety making her so clumsy she almost dropped it. She had flipped it open before her mind started to work and she closed it.

"Hannah?"

"You have to leave first."

"Leave? I'm not leaving you here—"

"You have to. I can tell the cops I came by for a visit. They can check me out all they want. But you, Jack, you're suddenly in the middle of too many crazy things. Rocks and bombs and if it gets out, even a kidnapping. Now a murder?"

"My ID has held up so far. I'm not leaving you here alone to cope."

"You have to. You're Aubrielle's bodyguard and you can't do that from a jail cell. Everything has changed."

"No," he said, staring deep into her eyes. "I will not

leave you. Don't you understand? Someone shot and killed Fran. They could still be here."

"But you—"

"No, Hannah. This isn't about me." He gestured at her phone. "Call the police."

"There have been two similar murders in the past few months," she said. "In fact, Fran was worried I was being targeted when I told her about feeling watched."

He looked into her eyes. "Do you honestly believe this is a coincidence?"

She wanted to, but no, how could she on the heels of everything else that had happened that day? She shook her head. "It looks like the killer tried to make it look like one of those murders." And, accepting the inevitable, she placed the call.

They retreated to wait in the truck where they hurriedly discussed the things they wouldn't be telling the cops. "No word of the kidnapping," Hannah said, making Jack promise to agree. She was already sick to her stomach that whoever had taken Abby and warned about taking her grandmother if the police were notified would see contacting them now as an act of defiance on her part. She could see no option, however. This was murder, it couldn't be kept a secret.

Within minutes, the scene went from one of deathly quiet to a three-ring circus as emergency vehicles with screeching sirens started to fill the cul-de-sac, spilling police and a bevy of other officials.

She and Jack were separated and asked to run through the discovery of Fran's body. Hannah recounted every detail she could recall, explaining that she'd come by to discuss work issues with Fran and that Jack had given her a ride as her car was in the shop.

All the time she answered questions her attention

was divided between the crime scene a dozen feet away, Aubrielle's growing discontent with her baby seat and her own worry about Jack. The police would talk to everyone at the Staar Foundation—Jack's name would come up as a man who had been with Fran that morning. His fingerprints were all over Fran's doors but they must also be all over the inside of Fran's house as he'd eaten dinner with her the night before.

She should have figured out a way to make him leave.

At last the detective asking questions seemed to notice the baby was at the end of her rope. "You can go now, Ms. Marks," he said, "but stay close by. We may have further questions."

He was a middle-aged man with receding blondish hair and an extra twenty pounds on his frame. The smell of his clothes identified him as a smoker.

"Is this the work of the garage killer?" Hannah asked as medics rolled a gurney past her to the ambulance. Hannah averted her eyes, unable to believe that Fran could really be inside that body bag, dead and gone from the world.

The detective shrugged.

"Can Jack Carlin leave now, too?" she asked, almost uttering Jack's real last name, but catching herself.

The detective glanced over at Jack. "Not yet. I'll get someone to give you and your baby a ride home."

"I'd rather call a cab," Hannah said. She wasn't sure she should mention the fact that she was staying with Jack in a hotel room in Fort Bragg. She felt sick with the stress of telling half-truths to say nothing of the shock of Fran's murder.

Jack met her gaze as she carried Abby out to the cab. She could almost read his mind: *Be careful, there's a murderer loose. You might be next on his list....*

Chapter Eleven

Jack gave the hotel as his temporary address and drove away an hour later, warnings of staying in town still ringing in his ears. He was a "person of interest" in the murder of Fran Baker. So far his identity was holding up, but it wouldn't for long; it wouldn't withstand serious investigation.

He'd had to tell the cops he was with Fran the night before. He'd had to tell them he'd visited her at work. He had no idea what they would make of all this but he could feel the noose tightening around his throat and if she'd kept the real estate card he'd given her the night before and they found it when they processed her house, he was going to have to try to explain why he'd lied to her.

Jail. Even if it was just long enough to straighten everything out, the prospect of captivity made him sweat. There was a huge part of him that just wanted to keep driving. To hell with Tierra Montañosa and Hannah and Aubrielle and Mimi and everyone else. Was finding the truth and maybe diverting a disaster worth the loss of his freedom?

He got back to the hotel, anxious to make sure Hannah and Abby had arrived safely. Even if he ran, he had to know they were okay first.

When he opened the door, he found Hannah sitting in a chair, head back, eyes closed. She'd apparently taken another shower because her hair was damp and she'd changed into soft gray slacks and a sweater. Her luscious lips reminded him of ripe fruit and he throbbed with the desire to kneel in front of her, kiss her, ravish her.

Abby was asleep on Hannah's lap, cheeks flushed pink, arms flung above her head.

He stared at them for a long moment, the doorknob still in his hand, one foot inside the room and the other still in the hall. And then he stepped all the way into the room and closed the door behind him. The click roused Hannah, whose eyes opened abruptly.

"Jack, I was so worried they would take you in for questioning—"

"That's probably what's coming next," he said. "I don't think we have much time, Hannah."

"Should we change hotels?"

"That would just make me look more guilty than I already do. No, there's no point. But tomorrow is sink-or-swim day. Tomorrow we make things happen. We're out of time."

"I know."

"I'm hitting the shower," he said.

"I'll call room service and order dinner."

Forty-five minutes later, they both pushed pasta and chicken around on their plates, too preoccupied by Fran's death to engage in conversation until Hannah finally laid aside her fork. "So, you don't think the police believe it was the garage killer?"

"I don't think so. They usually have details they don't share with the newspapers so they can tell if something is copycat. I'm just guessing here though."

"Did they mention how long she'd been dead?"

"I overheard the M.E. say something about more than three hours."

"Jack, I was thinking. What if Fran was the one blackmailing someone?"

"And that someone thought it was you?"

"Yeah."

"If that's true, then why did they kidnap Abby, threaten your grandmother? The killer couldn't have been everywhere at the same time. If Fran had been blackmailing someone, wouldn't that someone want what she had and wouldn't that have meant forcing her inside to get it? If she'd met with whoever it is away from home, then why trail her back to her garage to kill her?"

"To make it look like the garage killer."

"Maybe. I don't know, I just have a feeling we're missing something."

"The police will question the people at Staar, won't they?" Hannah said suddenly.

"I imagine."

"And some of them will mention she was with you, Jack. They might even know you were passing yourself off as a real estate agent."

"I know," he said.

Hannah's cell phone rang and she answered it. "Grandma," she said, and proceeded to listen. Jack closed his eyes and almost fell asleep in the chair.

She roused him with a gentle touch on his shoulder. "Grandma is fine. I'm exhausted."

No use pretending he wasn't. Hannah slept in the bed next to Aubrielle, Jack had the other bed to himself.

It was a big bed and it was lonely. Enough light filtered through the curtains that he could see the curve of Hannah's hip beneath her covers. He turned over to face the wall and shut his eyes, but the sensory over-load of the day had hunkered down deep in his psyche. Seeing the rags floating out at sea and thinking maybe, maybe it was Abby. Fran's obliterated face, the evening in the intimate setting of a motel room but without the intimacy, the indecision, the doubts...

It was almost enough to make a man miss the jungle.

Sometime later, he awoke with a start when he felt weight shift on the bed. Muscles tensed and he shot out a hand to grab whoever was there, reaching high for a throat. His fingers closed on petal-soft skin and he instantly withdrew his hand and swallowed.

Hannah...

Her fuzzy outline grew closer as a soft hand landed on his shoulder, warm breath caressed his cheek.

"What's wrong?" he sputtered.

She folded back the covers and slipped in beside him. She was naked, and the velvety slide of her warm skin next to his created an immediate physiological reaction. What was going on?

He must have asked it out loud, for she laughed against his shoulder. "Could I be any more obvious?" she whispered against his neck. The firm mounds of her breasts pressed against his side, her hip rested against his erection.

"Damn it, Hannah, this isn't fair," he said, keeping his voice as soft as hers.

"I know. I'm sorry." She didn't act sorry. Her fingers were currently entwined in his chest hair and her lips were inches away from his.

"It's been a year," he said. "If you're waiting for me to kick you out of bed and save you from yourself, you've come to the wrong man."

"A year? Since you and I—"

"Since me and anyone. There aren't any conjugal visits in a guerilla camp."

She was silent for a second. He turned slightly, slipping an arm under her head, burying his nose in her silky hair as it spilled over his skin. His body went up in flames.

"I almost died when I heard you were taken in Costa del Rio," she murmured. "And then when reports came that your body was identified—I didn't know it was just your watch. I thought you were gone forever, but here you are." Her lips brushed the corner of his mouth.

"Here we both are," he said. Her words had caressed his heart in a way he hadn't realized he'd needed. All those months in captivity, the deaths of the others, the hopelessness—he'd told himself no one would mourn him, would care, but his head had been full of images of Hannah, hopes that she might be thinking of him, might even hope she'd see him again someday....

Was that the real reason he'd come after her?

"Are you going to make me ask you?" she whispered, her hand moving south on his torso. Next stop: the point of no return. He caught her fingers.

"I'm not the kind of man you need, *cariño*," he muttered. Hell. He should have those words tattooed on his forehead. He should have them embossed in Braille on his chest. He should—

"You are exactly the man I need," she said so softly he more or less stopped breathing so he could hear her. "I want you, Jack. Just for tonight…"

Her voice trailed off and then she whispered, "Do you have any protection?"

"No," he said. "Do you?"

"No. But the last time either of us made love, it was with each other, right?"

"But pregnancy—"

"It's okay," she said. "I don't think I can get pregnant yet."

"*Cariño,* I happen to know that's bull."

She pulled her hand free and it landed with the most gentle stroke right where he knew it would, right where he'd been aching for her to touch, and that's when he threw in the mental towel.

IT WASN'T LIKE THE FIRST TIME they'd made love. It wasn't the all-consuming fire fueled by hours of flirting, tequila and foreplay, the desire so thick and steamy it had rivaled the humidity in the un-air-conditioned South American room.

But it was better. Longer. His attention to detail in pleasing her sending her places she hadn't known existed. Not at first. At first he was too far gone, she'd pushed him as far as she could or wanted to and he came into her with such need it drilled her to the bed. His release had thrilled her, empowered her, touched her somewhere so deep inside it frightened her. While their responses to each other were by necessity quieter than before because of Aubrielle's proximity in the other bed, they were no less earth-shaking.

The next time, he made it about her. Touching her, arousing her, his mouth everywhere, tasting her like she was a banquet, crushing her and lifting her and when her own need met his, coming to her again.

They fell asleep in each other's arms, waking when weak light made its way between the gap in the drapery. She'd wondered if she'd be embarrassed, wondered if he would, but she awoke to find him looking at her with such desire in his expression that parts of her melted anew.

She quickly glanced across at the other bed to make sure Aubrielle was still fast asleep. Cuddling close to Jack she murmured, "Morning," into his delightfully hairy chest.

His arms closed around her. "Morning. Want to take a shower and see what comes up?"

"Yes," she said, snuggling even closer. His intentions were clear and her body was already thrumming with anticipation. And then she came to her senses. She kissed his collarbone and wrapped her arms around him, pulling him as close as she could, loving the masculine feel of him pressed against her, the heat…

"I can't," she finally whispered. "Aubrielle will be waking up soon. Will you listen for her while I take a quick shower?"

"Of course," he said with another dozen kisses and a lingering hand on her rear that was hard to resist.

She felt his eyes on her as she got out of the bed and walked nude to the bathroom, remembering to suck in everything possible. Her breasts were fuller than the last time—nursing could do that—and she wondered what else had changed in a year. *Besides everything.*

She took a very quick shower, washing the last of Jack Starling from her skin. A night like the one they'd just spent would never happen again; it would be stupid to tempt fate and open herself to more heartache, but she'd been powerless to resist his pull the night before.

Oh, come off it, Hannah, she admonished herself as she pulled on her jeans. *He was sound asleep.*

But the truth was she'd awoken quite a while before she went to his bed. She'd lain there trying to figure things out, her brain still reeling with yesterday's nightmares, and she'd come up with an idea. She knew she owed it to Jack to run it by him, so she'd sat up in bed and watched his slumbering form and it had come to her that she didn't want to wake him with a half-baked plan he would want to argue with. But she did want to wake him; oh, how she wanted that.

Dare she?

She'd checked to make sure Aubrielle was out like a zombie and then she'd stood and pulled off her nightgown and taken a step and then a half step and she was there and the rest, well, the rest had been exactly what they both needed....

Okay, ideally it wouldn't have been so good, so fulfilling, gone so deep or meant so much. Ideally it wouldn't have lived up to the memory of the time before and she could have let him go with a lighter heart.

Fastening her hair into a knot at the back of her head, she was ready to face the day and something told her it was going to be a doozy.

Fran was dead, brutally murdered, and Hannah was positive she knew, maybe even liked, her killer. Harrison Plumber, bumbling on the outside, but maybe conniving on the inside. Old Santi Correa, gutted after his son's capture. Hugo Correa, who had returned from the jungle with a mangled leg. Gary Jenkins, a quiet bookkeeper-type guy with a family.

She knew Fran's killer, she just didn't know his name, not yet, anyway, but she would soon. The trick would be surviving the discovery.

HANNAH, HER VOICE SOUNDING totally reasonable, wound up by saying, "The trick will be getting their attention."

Jack had had to force himself to sit there and listen.

He kept expecting the police to knock on the door. All he wanted to do was get out of the hotel. "You mean showing enough to scare them into the open so we can identify them without causing them to sneak around the back and kill you?" he said dryly.

"More or less. My plan is to send e-mails to each of them. I tell them I have something they want and it's theirs for a price, meet me at the same place they left my baby yesterday. The note will only make sense to one of them and he'll be the one who shows up."

"And you're the bait."

"I guess, but you're the guy with the gun protecting the bait. Do you have a better plan?"

"Better? No. Different, yes. I want to talk to the man who killed David and I want to check out the cash David left. My only worry is how to keep you and Abby safe while I do it."

"I told you, her name is Aubrielle," Hannah said with a flash of irritation.

"Why is it so important to you?" he asked suddenly. "In a few days you'll never see me again."

He instantly regretted the words. Coming after the passionate night they'd just spent, they seemed cruel and unwarranted and yet there'd been a flavor of parting in their lovemaking he hadn't been able to deny and that had left him feeling uneasy. Or maybe it was just the fact that he could feel time ticking away…

She blinked a couple of times before stuttering, "It just is."

"Okay, Aubrielle it is. What do I do with you two while I go ask questions?"

"You drive us back to Allota. My car is ready and I want it."

"We're staying together until this is over. I'm the baby's bodyguard."

"Yeah? Well, I'm the baby's mother and I need my car. You do your thing, I'll do mine."

"But—"

"Jack, I am *not* going to wait around for whoever took Abby—damn, now you've got me doing it—whoever took Aubrielle to decide to do it again."

"If it was really Fran, then her death will stop it," he said.

"You know there's more to it than that."

What could he do? The baby wasn't his, he was just the hapless idiot trying to be a bodyguard in what was obviously an on-and-off-again proposition.

"We're ready," she said a moment later and he looked up to find her waiting in front of him, dressed head to toe in black. She looked sexy as hell. The only jarring note was the bundle of pink held tenderly in her arms and the watermelon diaper bag slung over one shoulder.

The fog of the day before had deteriorated into unabated rain. It took most of a half hour to get to Allota where they found Hannah's car restored to near new condition. Jack asked her to follow him back to Fort Bragg, but she declined by explaining she wanted to reassure the florist she'd alarmed the day before.

"Then promise me you'll meet at the mailbox place, say in two hours."

She rose on tiptoes to kiss the corner of his mouth. "I promise. Stop worrying."

"Just don't do anything…impulsive."

She didn't respond.

Chapter Twelve

The final version was short:

I know things. I have evidence. Meet me at 3:30 today where you left something dear to me yesterday. Bring the usual payment. Come alone.

She didn't sign it. One person would know it was her; she didn't want to admit her identity to those who would take the e-mail as some sick joke. Using an alternate Web site she'd set up months before for another purpose, she sent it anonymously on the library computer.

Her thinking was simple: either Fran's killer was the same person who had abducted Aubrielle and searched Hannah's house or he wasn't. Either way, this note should make his skin crawl. He would be driven to finding out what she knew or what she had. She was counting on it.

The e-mail was sent early so there would be plenty of time for any of the men to get to Allota, even Santi Correa from the Bay Area three hours south. He might be too sickly to drive himself, but he had a chauffeur. If it was him, he'd get here.

And Jack? He would be upset he hadn't been in on

the final decision, but he would come around. The one thing she knew was that he would never jeopardize her safety by agreeing to use her this way. If she presented it as a done deal, he'd have no choice.

She hit the button four times to send the four notes to the four men, and then she swooped up Aubrielle's car seat and the sleeping baby within and went back out into the rain. Next stop: Mimi's house. It looked abandoned although when she stepped inside, she could tell someone had been there. The shelves had been searched, closet doors left ajar, drawers open.

Had Fran's murderer walked these halls?

She knew she should turn tail and run, but the very fact that the search had been such a civilized one emboldened her. The house had an empty feeling now, anyway; whoever had done it was gone, she could feel it. She moved quickly, gathering the things she needed. Jack had the binoculars and she couldn't find another pair, but the rifle scope would work almost as well. A change of clothes, from black to grays. A knit hat to cover her hair.

It was a relief to lock the door behind her and Aubrielle.

Lastly, she drove to the florist's shop and parked in back behind the delivery van. Waiting until no one was around, she unhooked the baby's seat, grabbed the diaper bag and rushed through the back door of the shop, running into a very surprised Lindy, who was prepping flowers at the back station.

Lindy's expression went from startled to relieved. "Hannah! Are you okay? Yesterday was so odd. I tried calling but you weren't home."

Hannah took a deep breath and closed the outside

door. "Will you call Jill and ask her to meet me here? I need to talk to you both. I need help."

"WHO DID YOU SAY YOU ARE?" The wan-looking woman asking the question shifted a small child from one hip to the other.

"My name is Jack Carlin," Jack said, flashing his false ID one more time.

"And just exactly what do you want with Mitch?"

"I'm working for the dealership that sold him his truck last year, Mrs. Reynolds. They're doing a customer follow-up survey."

"Well, he's not here," she said. The kid on her hip wasn't very old but he looked solid and Mitch's wife was a scrawny kind of woman who appeared to need vitamin shots.

For all her fragility, however, she also possessed a kind of feral quality, made evident when she suddenly narrowed her eyes. "Would we get something for taking part in this survey?"

"It's worth twenty bucks," Jack said. He tried a warm smile and added, "Of course, that's not enough money to make a difference to people like you and your husband."

"What do you mean?" she snapped, whisking stray dark hair from her cheek. Overhead, the sagging roof of the porch strained under the relentless pounding of the rain. The Reynoldses lived on a dead-end street, which was damn poetic considering the dead-end feel of the place.

He gestured at the RV parked beside the house. "Well, people like you with expensive vehicles and—"

She snorted away his response. The kid apparently grew weary of clinging to her bones and struggled to get down. She put him on his feet and he ran off into the shadows of the house, screaming at the top of his lungs.

"Don't you believe it," she said, wilting against the doorjamb. "It cost an arm and a leg to fill the gas tank on that albatross. We only took it out once and then the economy turned and now we can't give it away. Mitch just had to have it, though. Okay, I'll take the survey."

"I'm sorry," he said. "It has to be Mitch because he signed the papers. Do you know when he'll be home?"

"He left yesterday morning on some errand and never bothered to come back. He better not be with those no-good friends of his." She cast Jack a longer look and kind of straightened herself up. "How about you, Mr. Carlin? You want to come inside and have a cup of coffee...or something?"

Jack did his best to look regretful. "I'm sorry, no time. Can you give me an idea of where I could find Mitch? I mean, isn't it unusual for him to stay out all night? Aren't you worried?"

"Yeah, it's unusual but these are hard times and he's been distracted lately—"

Her eyes narrowed again as suspicion curled her lip. "What the hell do you care if my husband stays out all night? Who are you?"

"I'll try to reach him at work," Jack said, backing up. "Ace Trucking, right?"

She stared at him a second, and then she laughed with a worn-down bitter shake of her head. "Damn it, you're scamming me, aren't you? He owes you money. That's why you're really looking for him, isn't it? Well, he got laid off two months ago and he hasn't worked a day since, so don't get your hopes up." With that, she slammed the door.

Jack drove away with a frown creasing his forehead. Could it be a coincidence that Mitch Reynolds disappeared on the same day Fran Baker was murdered? Probably. There was nothing to connect them except circumstance. Fran had been dating David and David had been killed by Mitch. Whether it was an accident, as he claimed, or murder was almost immaterial.

And that brought it back to the inevitable: the Staar Foundation.

He had plenty of time to meet Hannah and Abby, but some inner sense of urgency had him racing anyway. He wanted to have them both in sight. Nothing could happen to either one of them, he wouldn't let it, but that meant he had to be around, not off somewhere else. Hannah's independence was a giant pain in the neck but technically speaking, the baby was his client, not her sexy mom.

The roads on the north side of the bridge were little more than dirt and the tires on the old truck were hardly new. After a near spinout on a patch of gravel by the road leading off to the quarry, he slowed down.

A minute or two later, a police car sped by going the other direction, lights flashing but no siren. Jack pulled the truck to the side of the road and turned in his seat to stare back at the cruiser, curious if it would continue on to the Reynoldses' place. The sudden whine of an approaching siren had him whipping around in his seat again, this time to find another police car and behind it, an ambulance. Both roared past him going ninety miles an hour. All three vehicles showed brake lights as they turned left some distance behind him.

Nothing to do with Mitch Reynolds and his pathetic wife.

And yet...

Get yourself out of here, you fool. The thought was so strong Jack could almost hear the words. And then he thought of Fran and Hannah and Abby. He had to know what was going on and how it would affect them.

He found a wide spot to turn around and cautiously retraced the distance, turning left where he'd seen the cops and ambulance turn. A beat-up old sign by the side of the road promised a rock quarry in a mile. He knew he should stop and turn around and yet he couldn't.

Trees crowded the pavement while mysterious overgrown driveways barred with rusted chains and posted with No Trespassing signs disappeared into the undergrowth. When he could see the road was going to terminate in the quarry he slowed way down. After all the greenery, the old excavation site looked like a moonscape.

Jack turned onto a spur that ran parallel to the quarry, shielded by a curtain of fir trees. A hundred feet farther along, the new road provided a good spot for camouflage almost directly opposite where all the action seemed to be concentrated. He peered through the rain-spattered windshield for a few seconds until he remembered the binoculars he'd taken from Hannah's house the day before when they went to find Aubrielle. He dug them out from behind the seat.

The quarry had obviously been abandoned years before. Equipment stood frozen in place, victims of time and neglect. The few buildings still standing leaned precariously. Where the earth had been gouged away, sinister dark pools of water had collected.

In the middle of all the gloom, the emergency vehicles

and milling humans looked almost cheerful. In addition to the cops and the ambulance, there was also a newer white car from which a teenage couple scrambled. The girl produced a red umbrella that she opened over their heads. A cop approached them and began writing in a notebook as they spoke. Jack recognized the detective from Fran's house.

Great.

The kids couldn't take their gazes from the pool of water less than ten feet away. Try as he might, Jack couldn't see clearly enough through the rain to make out what had grabbed everyone's attention in that bitter-looking water, but it didn't take a mind reader to get strong vibes that something bad was going down.

Two more vehicles arrived in the next couple of minutes. One was an industrial tow truck manned by no-nonsense-looking men and the other was a police accident response van towing a boat. Diving equipment appeared from the van. The ambulance crew retreated back to the ambulance to wait.

Additional cars arrived, and more personnel gathered. It took most of thirty minutes for one diver to enter the water and return empty-handed. During that time, Jack got out of the truck. A lull in the rain gave him a chance to stretch his legs and quell the rolling tension in his stomach. The diver eventually went in again, this time guiding the winch and cable from the tow truck. Sometime later, the water roiled and a long, green sedan began to emerge trunk first from the murky depths.

Jack stood glued to the spot, binoculars held tight against his face. The ambulance crew emerged, moving in slow motion, opening the back of their vehicle, releasing the gurney, in no particular hurry. Meanwhile, every breath seemed suspended, every eye trained on the car as it rolled out of the water and settled on the slag, water pouring from every door frame and cracked window.

The car was a celery-green luxury model circa 1960, built back when most American cars were actually American products, the kind with tailfins on the fenders. He'd seen it or one just like it somewhere recently.

Eventually, the doors were opened and a body recovered. For some reason Jack assumed it would be an old man, maybe with a bad back. He lowered the binoculars with a puzzled expression on his face when he saw enough to realize the victim was male, but hardly old.

He looked again.

Red hair plastered to his skull, white sweatshirt with the New Orleans Saints' NFL logo on the front. A hole in the middle of his forehead made a third, deadly eye.

With a shock, Jack recognized the victim: it was the guy from the parking lot from the day before. The guy driving the hatchback. Different car, same man...

It was time, way past time, to get away and Jack got back in his truck. Hopefully the rain would cover the noise of the engine starting.

His mind raced backward like a film on rewind. Where had he seen the car? Why had he associated it with an old man and a cane? "Think, Jack!" he said, hitting the steering wheel with his fist, and that jarred him, as well; it somehow fit with the old guy and the green car—

The supermarket parking lot his first day in town. Hannah hitting the horn with her fist, the old man tapping on her window, asking if she was okay, walking off all bent over with a cane—

The contents of the hatchback flashed through his head. The wooden dowel could easily have been a portion of a cane. There'd been a folded raincoat, too. And a fedora—an old guy's hat.

What was going on? Who was this man and how was he involved with Hannah? That he was involved was clear—he'd been in the parking lot when she complained she felt "watched," wearing the disguise of an elderly man. He'd showed up at the car park when Aubrielle was taken.…

Okay, okay, what did Mitch Reynolds have to do with this? Could it be a coincidence he didn't come home on the same day Fran Baker was killed, the same day, probably, anyway, that the guy in the Saints sweatshirt ended up dead in a quarry less than two miles from the Reynolds house?

Did the same gun kill both victims?

A cold sweat broke out on Jack's forehead. He made himself drive slowly, relieved beyond words when an outlet to the main road appeared a good distance farther along than the one the police would use.

The cops would identify the guy in the quarry and start tracing his movements backward. They would question the Staar Foundation employees and the guy at the front desk would reveal Fran had brought a visitor the day she died, name of Jack Carlin. If Mitch Reynolds was implicated, they would question Mrs. Reynolds and she would tell them about Jack Carlin asking questions. Word would get back to Allota and the cop who had flirted with Hannah would remember she'd had a friend with her when her car was bombed, a friend with a Harley parked by her house, name of Jack Carlin.

And hey, wasn't it Jack Carlin, who along with Hannah Marks, found a dead woman yesterday after spending the evening before inside her house?

He'd thought he had this one day to figure things

out and now he wasn't sure he even had that. The possibility of ending up a guest of the California penal system wasn't much more comforting than the thought of reuniting with his terrorist buddies in the GTM.

Movement in the rearview mirror caught his attention. Flashing lights, a siren…

He pulled to the side of the road, praying the cop would keep going, but the police unit pulled in behind him.

Jack braced his hands on the wheel and fought the urge to gun the engine and try to outrun the cop. He took a deep breath, centering himself, thinking of Hannah. He had to stay free in order to find her and Abby and protect them. Hannah could be his focus, his anchor, at least for today.

He carefully swept the flashlight under the seat. The shotgun behind the seat was hidden from view. True, he was less than a half a mile away from a murder scene but there was no law against driving down this road. The bigger issue was Hannah, who was unaware another body had showed up. Aubrielle was vulnerable; him getting caught in the legal system might endanger them both. He would be calm.

Still, if he made it through the day without being hauled off to jail, it would be a miracle.

HANNAH SHOWED UP AT THE commercial mailboxes a little late but there was no sign of Jack. With Aubrielle asleep against her shoulder and wrapped in blankets against the chill, she stood under the awning for a while, growing increasingly impatient, glancing at her watch every few seconds.

Where was he? He couldn't still be at the Reynoldses' house. She needed him, she'd counted on him. Now that her plan was in motion, there were things she needed to be doing and they didn't include twiddling her thumbs.

It wasn't like Jack to be late.

A shiver of apprehension ran through her chest. Had he run into trouble? Had he gone off on a wild hair?

All that was for certain was that he was late and she was counting on him to cover her, sure he'd be willing once he discovered she'd gone ahead and sent the e-mails. It was a good plan. Not very subtle, but good. Even the pounding rain worked to her advantage as it would obscure things a little. She could almost hide behind the raindrops.

Of course, then, so could whoever showed. Someone she knew—someone who was willing to endanger a baby and kill a woman...

It suddenly dawned on Hannah that she'd managed to disenfranchise Fran the woman from Fran the corpse. Maybe belief and horror would have set in that morning if she'd gone into work and been confronted by Fran's empty office, the lingering scent of her perfume, her coworkers shocked and grieving. Those things would have brought it home.

Fran had been brutally murdered and Hannah had just invited the murderer to meet her. There was no way to pretend that was a good idea. Jack was right, it was too risky.

Think. What did she do if she didn't carry through with her plan? Run away like she'd made her grandmother run?

No, no, she couldn't get cold feet, she couldn't live in fear, couldn't raise a child in fear. She had to figure this out. Jack might be worried about innocent lives in Tierra Montañosa and she was, too, but the truth was, she was more worried about the life she was solely responsible for right here and now.

After an eternity of pacing and growing unease, she got back in her car and drove away. Hedging her bets, she went out of her way to stop by the hotel and checked out their room to make sure Jack hadn't gone back there for some reason, but the room was as they had left it; the maid hadn't even changed the towels or made up the bed yet. Hannah fed and changed the baby, hoping Jack would show up any second, watching the door as though she could will him to open it. Eventually, she gave up, but as she stood, she caught sight of the bed she'd shared with him. Memories of the night's sensations swirled through her brain. Would memories of him be enough to take into the future?

The future. Here she was worrying about the future when her energies would be far better spent getting through today. She scribbled a note on the hotel stationery warning Jack to stay away from the car park this afternoon and left the room. Several minutes later, for the second time that day, she parked behind Lindy's store.

Unbuckling Aubrielle's car seat, she flung a blanket over the top to keep the rain off, grabbed the diaper bag and made a dash for the door, the baby screaming at the top of her lungs.

Lindy's grown daughter met her at the door. Jill was only two years older than Hannah but already had three children under the age of five. After a quick hug for Hannah, Jill swept baby and car seat away. Aubrielle was free of constraint a few seconds later, all tears gone.

"Sorry I couldn't get away until now," Jill said as she kissed Aubrielle. "I just dropped the kids off at the fire station with their daddy. He's off duty today but there's the annual picnic, moved inside because of this weather. Mom filled me in on the phone. You'll pick Aubrielle up at our place?"

"Yes." Hannah handed phone numbers to Jill, both hers and her grandmother's. "Grandma is traveling and my ringer will be off for a while but the vibrator will be on. It might take me a few minutes to call you back though, okay?"

"Sure, no problem. Hey, remember, please, I was a nurse before I became mother earth and my husband is a fireman so there's not too much that can happen one of us can't handle. Anyway, we'll be at the station for a while, and that's full of people who know how to cope with emergencies. You just concentrate on your hush-hush job interview."

"Thanks," Hannah said, wishing she hadn't had to lie.

Jill lowered her voice. "Does your switching jobs have something to do with that murder?"

"Murder?"

"That woman, Francis Baker, the one who worked out where you do at the foundation. The newspaper said it was the garage killer but my husband says his buddy on the force says the MO is wrong."

"Nothing to do with that," Hannah said, resisting the urge to grab her baby back and run for the hills.

"Oh."

"Did you hear about the other murder?" Lindy said.

"What other murder?"

"It was on the radio a few minutes ago. They found Brace Tyson dead in his car at the old quarry. A couple of teenagers saw his car in the water."

"Brace, really?" Jill said, her eyes registering shock. "Are you sure they said he was murdered, Mom?"

"They called it 'suspicious circumstances.'"

Hannah said, "Who is Brace Tyson?"

"He was ahead of me a couple of years in school so you probably missed him entirely," Jill said. "He moved to Los Angeles after graduation and came back here a year or two ago to start his own business, Tyson Investigation. You probably saw his office at the old strip mall south of town. He was a nice guy."

A private detective's body had been found out by the rock quarry where Jack had gone to talk to Mitch Reynolds? And now Jack was incommunicado? Uh-oh. Had the police caught up with him?

Hannah's stomach took another ride on a roller coaster as she glanced at her watch. There was no time to do anything but go to the beach and get ready for whomever showed up. Jack would have to figure this out on his own. Besides, she was jumping to conclusions— there was no proof Jack was involved in any way. Maybe his beat-up old truck broke down.

She reached over and touched Aubrielle's tiny fingers.

Jill cast her a soft look. "Don't worry, Hannah, she'll be fine, just like she was when I covered for your grandma. I'll take good care of her. We love babies at our house, you know that."

Hannah forced taut facial muscles into a smile. She could see by the way Lindy and Jill exchanged quick glances that she wasn't really putting anything over on either one of them. They knew something was up and they probably knew it wasn't a job interview. With a last hug for her baby, Hannah left.

Her first stop was the library. Once again she logged

on to their computer, this time holding her breath as she checked the e-mail account she'd used to send the messages hours before.

One response, but it was like landing the biggest fish in the lake, though the sender had disguised the e-mail's origins just as she had.

I'll be there. This has to stop.

Chapter Thirteen

Jack talked fast and furious. The cop seemed distracted, like he was only half listening to Jack's tale of getting lost while searching for the main road. Chances were the dead body in the car was the first one the young officer had ever encountered. Death, especially violent death, had a sobering effect.

"I got lost on all these little country roads. They all look the same in the rain. Say, I saw the emergency vehicles, even watched for a few minutes. Did someone get hurt?"

The cop, who looked cold and miserable but didn't seem to notice that Jack was also wet, didn't answer. Instead he studied Jack's temporary registration and his license, finally handing everything back with a grunt.

"You need to drive up this road about a mile and then turn right," he said. "Go straight three miles, turn right again, go straight into Fort Bragg. Better stay off these roads. Something like this isn't a spectator sport."

"Thank you, Officer." Jack did everything but hug the kid and drove off with a feeling of having escaped the grim reaper.

Hannah wasn't at the mailbox place, which surprised him. Where else did she have to be? Worried about showing up at the hotel if the police were watching for him, he stopped at a pay phone with that most scarce of commodities, an actual intact phone book. He called Hannah's cell number from memory first—no answer. Then he called the hotel and asked for their room. Batting zero, he called the florist in Allota.

"Lindy's Flowers and Gifts," a woman answered.

Jack identified himself, then added, "I'm a friend of Hannah Marks. I was supposed to meet her, but I got held up. Do you happen to know where she is?"

"She mentioned your name, Mr. Carlin, said you were the only one besides her grandmother who I should talk about the baby with. She left a little while ago to go on a job interview."

Job interview? He said, "Did she take Abby with her? I mean, Aubrielle?"

"Actually, my daughter is watching the baby. In fact, she has her at the fire station with the rest of her family. Hannah told me to tell you to stay away from the car park if you called after two-thirty and since it's almost three, I'm passing that message along."

"Thanks," he said. Back in the truck, he took off for Allota. Abby might be in good hands, but he'd bet the ranch Hannah was meeting with a murderer. No way was he sitting that out.

IT HAS TO STOP.

The words kept echoing in Hannah's head. They were the words she'd been saying over and over to herself that day. It was haunting to have them said to her and probably by a killer.

Originally, she'd thought to meet face-to-face with whichever man showed up in the beach car park, Jack covering her from behind a rock. But with Jack AWOL, that plan was too dangerous. She could not leave Aubrielle alone in the world by risking herself. The man coming today had probably killed Fran, maybe he'd killed David, maybe even the private eye whose body was found at the quarry. She would not be his next victim.

All she needed was an identity although proof would come in handy, as well. They could take that to the cops along with news of everything that had happened. It would be over.

She drove past the car park and up the adjoining hillside, looking for the dirt track that took off across the headland and wrapped its way back to overlook the beach. She'd ridden her bike along it often as a kid as it was the access to the rock castle. The rain made finding it tricky, but there it was at last.

She parked well back from the crest of the hill and walked in the rest of the way, head bent against the rain, her grandfather's hunting rifle with the scope gripped in one cold, wet hand. She'd taken the rifle because of the attached scope, knowing she could use it to sight something if need be. Her grandfather had taught her how when she was a teen. But with Jack's absence, the rifle also gave her a sense of security. Could she shoot someone if she had to? Hell, yes. The rifle was loaded and ready to go.

Thrust up through the earth's crust in the distant seismic past, the towering rocks dominated the top of the hill. In the right light and from the sea, they were sometimes mistaken for an actual man-made structure. They provided a bevy of hiding places both for a child's imagination and a grown woman with big problems.

Hannah found a spot where she could wiggle in under a slab of rock and look directly down on the beach parking lot. There were several cars in the lot, scattered here and there as people shared rides into town. For all Hannah knew, the man she awaited was already down there, waiting.…

She searched each vehicle, keeping an eye out for Hugo Correa's white Cadillac, Gary Jenkins's red Volvo, Harrison Plumber's blue SUV or Santi Correa's sky-blue Mercedes.

None of them were down there.

For most of twenty minutes, no new cars turned into the car park, which wasn't surprising given the intensity of the rain. She checked her watch again and again. The minutes were lazy, stretching instead of racing. She got a cramp in her leg. A gap between the rocks sent a steady trickle of cold water down her neck where it snaked along her spine, giving her newfound respect for the misery of water torture.

When a vehicle finally turned into the park, Hannah jerked in anticipation. Being a black van with tinted windows, it fit none of the suspects' cars. Maybe another tourist needing a rest stop. Or maybe the man she was looking for had brought a different vehicle.

The van parked one row back from the bathrooms, facing the exit. Hannah held her breath as a figure got out of the van, but as the driver's door was on the other side, she couldn't tell who it was. The figure moved around to the back of the van, moving slowly despite the rain. Hannah looked through the scope as the person walked clear of the van.

Steel-gray slicker, black broad-brimmed hat, dark glasses, gloves. Black pants showing from beneath the hem, black boots. Cautious gait, no hair showing. All she could tell for sure was that the person was acting suspicious, looking this way and that, slinking toward the bathrooms.

The newcomer walked into the women's room, back out and into the men's, then stood outside, apparently taking a reprieve from the rain by standing beneath the slanted metal overhang of the building. Hannah wasn't positive this person had anything to do with her. She couldn't identify the figure by what she could see although she had the impression it was a male. Even size was difficult to gauge from the distance and through the rain.

And then a movement off to the east caught her quarry's attention. Hannah lowered the scope to look toward the car park entrance where an old truck was rambling through the gate.

Jack. Damn...

She looked back at the bathrooms. The driver of the black van was gone. Hannah stretched out from her hiding spot a little, searching the car park as Jack came to a halt beside the van.

Where had the driver gone?

Jack got out of the truck, folded the seat forward and withdrew the shotgun. For a second, he stood by the truck, looking around. His mouth moved and she knew he was calling her name. She wiggled free of the rocks and was in the act of standing when a movement by the bathrooms caught her attention. Grabbing the rifle, she aimed it in order to bring the scope into range.

The person in the gray slicker had moved to stand behind the bathrooms, out of sight of Jack. There was no law against that, but why would someone act that way if they weren't expecting trouble? She was about to look for Jack again when she saw the gloved hand dip into a pocket of the slicker and bring out a silver revolver which he or she raised.

Where was Jack? Frantically, she looked around and

found him approaching the bathrooms. From where he was, he would not be able to see that someone held a gun on him. If he made a false move, would the armed person panic and fire? What should she do?

After ducking into each room, Jack stood with his hands on his waist, staring around, standing in almost the exact spot the other person had stood less than two minutes before.

The person with the gun inched closer, gun raised.

Hannah did the only thing she could think to do. She yelled.

Nobody heard her. The rain was too loud on the metal above Jack's head, she was too far away. The gunman moved closer to the building, obscuring Hannah's view. A second later, she saw a glint of the overhead bathroom light reflect off the end of the muzzle as it peeked out from behind cinder blocks. It was pointed right at Jack.

She raised the rifle. She hadn't shot it in years, wasn't sure how precise her aim was. The distance between Jack and the side of the building behind which his assailant lurked was less than eight feet. If she missed the building she could hit Jack.

She decided to fire at the van. Shattering a window would create a loud noise that would warn Jack.

The bullet hit the rear window of Jack's truck instead of the van but it had an effect.

Jack immediately ducked into the shadow of the building, shotgun aimed straight up the bluff—at her. She could read his indecision though she couldn't see his expression clearly. He'd expected trouble and she'd given it to him and the side effect of that was that he'd identified the danger—only it was misguided. No way the shotgun could hurt her from that distance, but what had happened was that his back was open to the real threat.

The thought had no more than skittered into her head than the gunman reappeared, his movements covered by the sound of the rain. He jabbed his revolver into Jack's back. Jack slowly dropped the shotgun. She could tell they were talking though Jack was apparently told to keep looking ahead of him. The gunman clearly didn't like Jack's answers. His movements became jerky, his anger telegraphing all the way up the bluff.

Hannah squeezed the trigger again, her intent being to hit the Dumpster. The shot went wild but it was apparently enough to get the assailant's attention, for he seemed to cut his losses. As he turned to run, the wind caught the brim of his hat and blew it off his head. Hannah gasped in recognition. As Jack scrambled for the shotgun, the gunman climbed into the van. Hannah fired again, but the van kept going.

By now Jack had reached his truck but he didn't get far in hot pursuit. The second or third bullet had apparently taken out a tire, maybe two. He got out of the truck, perused his tires and swore. Well, Hannah wasn't positive he swore, but it sure looked as though he did. He raised his gaze and looked up at the rocks. Hannah flipped on the safety and held the rifle above her head, then she turned and ran back to her car. She drove as fast as she could to the car park, arriving within a few minutes.

Jack, soaked through to the skin, stood by his lop-sided truck watching her approach with anxious eyes. He held the rain hat in his hands.

"Are you okay?" she asked as the window rolled down.

He grabbed the door and peered in at her. "I'm fine. Are you okay?"

"Yes, yes. Jack, I know who it was. The wind blew

his hat off. It was Hugo Correa, Jack. And he limped away after he bent over you. I can hardly believe it, but I got a good look. I don't know what he wants, but—"

"I recognized his voice. He wants a tape. That's what he said when he poked that gun in my back. 'Where is she? Where's the tape?'"

"What tape?" Hannah gasped.

"I don't know."

"The only tapes—"

"Are the ones you forgot to send to David's mother." He ran around the car and jumped in. "Let's go."

JACK KNEW THE MINUTE he walked into Mimi's house that someone had been there before them. "We may be too late," he said as he glanced at the pulled-out drawers and open cabinets.

"I don't think so. It was this way this morning when I came for Grandpa's rifle. If they'd found what they wanted, why try to bash you at the car park?"

He kept his mouth clamped shut. She may well have saved his life just now, but she'd come into a house that was compromised without him and set everything in motion—again without him. Some bodyguard he was turning out to be.

The box was in the closet right where they'd left it. If it didn't hold the right tape, he had no idea where to turn next.

"I forgot about the VCR tapes," she said as they dug through the contents. "Grandma has an old player hooked up to her bedroom television. Come on."

Carrying the box, they continued down the hall to Mimi's bedroom. Jack squelched when he walked—his clothes were hopelessly wet, right down to his shoes, but there was no way he was going to risk taking the time to dry things. If the police decided to look for either one of them, this was the second place they would come.

If Hugo Correa decided to come out in the open, he knew where Hannah lived....

The wedding tape played on as Hannah disappeared to change clothes. She returned after a few minutes wearing the black outfit she'd started the day in.

"This is all I can offer," she said, handing him wool socks.

"Better than nothing. So far the tape is just a wedding," he added as he took off his shoes, peeled off his socks and put on the dry ones.

"Can we fast-forward?" she asked.

"I don't see why not." He handed her the remote and pulled on his boots, then he dug through the box for the audio tapes. "This could take hours we don't have. We can stop if something looks suspicious. Do you have an audiotape player, Hannah?"

"In the car."

There were five classical tapes, several pop, some heavy metal and even an opera or two. Some were home-recorded with titles and artists written in indelible ink on the plastic boxes. They were probably the best bets and when he got his hands on a player, he'd try those first. Unfortunately, there was no label marked "blackmail tape."

Hannah pulled out the wedding tape and popped in the flying lesson.

Jack, growing impatient, paced. When Hannah's phone rang, he took over the VCR duties. On the screen, a blue and white Cessna touched down on the tarmac and a few moments later, lens zooming in for a close-up, David waved from the window.

The tape went into static that he fast-forwarded

through just in case something had been recorded afterward. Hannah finished her phone conversation. "Grandma is in a town called Ferndale at a B & B having a ball."

"We need to take the audio tapes and get out of here," Jack said.

"Let me call Jill first. It'll only take a second."

She was true to her word, conducting the briefest of conversations. "Jill said the baby is awake and staring at her two-year-old. She says I can leave her there forever."

"And you told her no thanks."

"I told her I might have to take her up on an extended visit. She said that would be fine."

"There's no need for that. In fact, go to her now. Stay at Jill's house until I figure this out."

"No way. This is about my family being attacked by people I thought were my friends. I just can't wrap my head around Hugo Correa entering this house and stealing my baby. I can hardly believe it."

Jack knew what she meant. He didn't know Hugo well, but he'd been the man's bodyguard down in Tierra Montañosa for a few days, and he'd been left with the impression of a soft-spoken man who had always been in his father's shadow. He'd also seen him in the guerilla camp, witnessed a guard whacking his face with the butt of an automatic weapon. Hard to believe someone could live through all that and then be so cavalier with other people's lives.

He put an arm around Hannah and drew her closer. "Hannah, listen to me. Abby needs you. You're all she has. I don't have anyone depending on me. If I die, I die doing what I'm supposed to be doing, guarding you and her. But if something happens to either of you—"

He stopped because she'd pulled his head down and planted her mouth on his. He tasted the same longing on her lips as he did on his own. He ran his fingers along her throat as he lost himself in the sensation of kissing her. He wished for time, wished for peace, wished for the future in a way he'd never wished before.

She broke the connection and whispered into his neck, "What were you singing to Aubrielle the other day?"

"The lullaby? It's called 'Duerme, Niño Chiquito.'"

"What are the lyrics?"

"Let me think. *Sleep, my little baby,*" he began softly, his breath rustling her hair. "*Sleep, my little babe, sleep, my...precious soul,* I think that's right. *Sleep all through the night, my little morning star.*"

She was quiet for a long time and then she abruptly switched gears again. "I forgot to tell you something. The police found a dead private eye out at the rock quarry."

"I know, I was there when they pulled him out of the water and heard about his identity on the radio. A cop stopped me afterward, so the fact I was there is now on record."

"Great. What if the private eye was working for Hugo? Maybe he was the one watching me and skulking around my house."

"I wouldn't be surprised," Jack said. "Let's listen to these tapes."

THEY HUSTLED OUT TO HANNAH'S car. She automatically got behind the wheel.

"Drive a few blocks, just get away from this house," he told her. After she'd put a half mile between her grandmother's house and the car, she pulled up against the curb.

"Let's start with heavy metal," he said. "One of those that look like they were home-recorded." He slipped the tape into the tape player. "We'll fast forward through them all, pausing every few seconds to see if David taped over something. If nothing shows up, we can listen from beginning to end."

She suppressed a groan. There were hours of music on the tapes and they might be looking in the wrong place; these tapes might be totally immaterial. Maybe they should just go to the police and turn in Hugo.

She took the box and looked through the tapes, pausing for a second with the classical. While Black Sabbath crashed and banged in the background, she perused the artists. Mozart, Chopin, Beethoven.

"Jack?" she said slowly and when he didn't respond, turned down the radio volume. "Jack, do you still have that piece of paper I gave you, the one that was in the gym bag with David's money?"

"In my wallet," he said, digging his wallet out of his pocket. The leather was still damp but the paper he withdrew seemed dry. "9D 125 1-2," he read.

Looking at the plastic case in her hand, she said, "Beethoven's Symphony No. 9 in D Minor, Opus 125, Movements 1-2.

His lips curled into a smile. "That's it."

He ejected Black Sabbath and she popped in Beethoven and turned the volume back up. Violins filled the car. Hannah hit the fast-forward button for a second and resumed play. Trumpets, flutes and drums. She did this two additional times before the sound of men's voices replaced the music. They were speaking Spanish too fast for Hannah to follow and there was a lot of background noise confusing the issue further.

She looked at Jack as she juggled the buttons until the precise moment the music stopped abruptly and a man's voice whispered, "April 30, 11:20 a.m., Correa and Hurtado, Tierra Montañosa border, aboard Bell charter N480EX."

A shiver ran down Hannah's spine. It was jarring to hear David's guarded whisper after all this time and though a Spanish conversation in the background became the focal point, she could still hear David's excited breathing.

"Do you recognize Hugo's voice or the man David called Hurtado?" Jack asked her.

"No. I've never heard of anyone named Hurtado, either. They're speaking Spanish and it's like they're talking in a tin box."

"Must be aboard the helicopter," Jack said.

She pictured David on the chartered Bell. Maybe he'd been the pilot, maybe that's why they'd taken him to Ecuador so he could pilot a helicopter to a secret rendezvous. Maybe he was listening to the symphony when he caught wind of a business meeting in the back. David understood Spanish. Maybe he'd realized he was sitting on a gold mine if he could just record what he was hearing and use it to blackmail.

Jack turned the volume up and listened very carefully for several minutes as she sat there trying hard not to distract him. The tape suddenly went back to the music.

Jack turned off the player. She met his gaze. His eyes looked grim.

"What is it?" she asked. "What were they talking about?"

He rubbed his eyes. "I think David caught them in the middle of a conversation. They were plotting the ambush, they even talked about drugging me. Damn, remember how we both overslept? Hugo was staying in the same hotel. Maybe he paid someone to doctor the wine we ordered late that night."

She remembered the woozy way she'd felt upon wakening. It hadn't lasted long. When she'd shaken Jack awake and they both realized how late they were, there hadn't been time for woozy. "Yes, Hugo was staying there. We all were staying there. We were all on the same floor."

"I don't think the GTM was actually involved in the ambush. It sounded like the other guy, Hurtado, like he was in charge of creating a group that would claim to be the GTM, that would blame the ambush and everything else on them."

"Why would they do that?"

"To get the insurance money and have the credit go to the GTM who must have accepted the blame even though they didn't actually do anything because it fit their agenda."

"Hugo Correa shot himself?"

"No, I don't think so. I doubt he was meant to be hurt. It must have been an accident, something must have gone wrong when they staged their supposed release. Or maybe the other guy, Harrison Plumber, maybe he was suspicious so Hugo took one for the team. You said it yourself the other day, the company only insured the top echelon—to get all the money, they needed both Correa and Plumber."

"Then the Staar Foundation isn't backing the GTM."

"No, they're backing their own phony look-alike

group. They also mentioned something they called the 'thirtieth anniversary plans.' It sounded like something was in the offing for that day, too."

"That would be the day after tomorrow," Hannah said. "We have to go to the police."

He stared at her. "We have two days. Will the local cops listen, especially to me? Will they call in the Feds immediately? Will they take our word this tape is legit?"

Or would Jack be hauled off to jail as a person of interest in a murder or maybe two...?

"Santi Correa," she said.

"What about him?"

"He has all the connections. He can stop the celebrations with one phone call. God, the governor will be here and a senator or two. Why would the they want to hurt anyone here? What good would it do for some bogus group a half a world away?"

"I have no idea," he said. "Maybe there'll be another ransom."

"Santi is coming tomorrow afternoon for Sunday's open house but that's too late. We could call him...."

"You can't tell a man his son is destroying his life's work over a telephone. How long would it take to drive to his house?"

"Three hours, maybe four."

"I'll go," he said.

"I'll go with you."

"But Aubrielle—"

"It's too dangerous to take her."

"Please stay with her," Jack said, gripping her hands. "I can imagine how you feel knowing David chose to make money off this mess instead of blowing the whistle. It's a hell of a legacy for him to pin on little Abby, and trust me, I know a thing or two about fathers who do terrible things and leave their kids to live with the consequences. My own father pulled one of those. Let me make this right for her. You stay safe."

Tears burned behind Hannah's nose as she looked into Jack's eyes. Aubrielle's real father was a man of honor and bravery, not a scheming coward like David—she'd never wanted more to tell Jack the truth.

"Trust me," he said.

"I do trust you," she assured him but that was a lie. She might trust him with her life but she didn't trust him with her daughter—*his daughter, too.* "It's not just about me and Aubrielle anymore, Jack. It never was but I refused to believe it. Santi might not listen to you or even agree to see you, but he will see me. It's the only way."

"Then she comes with us," he said.

"I don't know, Jack."

"I'm her bodyguard. Bad things happen when we split up. We all go or I go alone."

Despite the fact his truck was in pieces down at the beach—something she was directly responsible for—and she had the only drivable car around, his ultimatum made its point. He was right. Bad things happened when they were apart.

But sometimes bad things happened when they were together, too.

Chapter Fourteen

The first thing to do was to establish that Santi Correa was actually at his home. There was a good chance he might have left early to attend the festivities, especially seeing as his employee, Fran Baker, was killed the day before. If he was growing frail, he might have given himself a little extra time for the trip.

Had the police asked him questions about Fran? Had Hugo said anything to his father to cover his guilt? Hannah didn't know what to expect.

But Santi made no mention on the phone of the extraordinary events of the past couple of days and sounded as reasonable as ever, as though he'd had no communication with anyone about what had been going on. That begged the question—would he really be able to help?

What other choice was there?

"I'll be most pleased to see you whenever you arrive," Santi assured her in his formal way.

They picked up Aubrielle a short while later. Thanks to Jill, the baby was fed and washed but she wasn't quite ready to go to sleep. Jack took the wheel so Hannah could keep an eye on her daughter and that meant numerous attempts to distract her with rattles and pacifiers and songs. Hannah was reaching between the two seats as often as she was facing forward. The fact the baby's back was to her didn't help, nor did the dark.

"David knew," she said at one point, turning to sit down and face forward. Her stomach lurched, a combination of nerves, looking backward in a moving vehicle and shock. "He knew they were going to kill people and he did nothing. I can't believe it."

"But he did *do* something," Jack said. "He told Correa he knew what was going on and Correa paid him the hush money David subsequently gave to you. That must be how it happened."

"And then Hugo got former employee Mitch to kill David and make it look like an accident."

"And somehow Fran knew or guessed," Jack said. "At least, that's kind of the way it looks."

"Fran's new car, even her decision to move to a fancier house all kind of point to an influx of cash, as though she'd continued blackmailing Hugo," Hannah said. "If she and David were having an affair, he might have told her the truth of what he heard and what he'd done. Maybe Fran's been trying to find the money, maybe she broke into my apartment."

"Or maybe she wanted to find the tape if David admitted to her there was one."

"Fran and David were both willing to overlook mass murder," Hannah said. "I haven't exactly been a good judge of character lately, have I?"

"Oh, I don't know," he said, sparing her a glance. "Jill seemed like a nice lady and of course, there's me to consider."

She smiled into the dark but it was a bittersweet smile. Just that morning, after they'd made love half the night, he'd reminded her he'd be gone when this was over. He wasn't the permanent type; he'd warned of that many times.

"Take the next left," she said, directing Jack to the cutoff for the road connecting the coast road to the less twisty Highway 101 several miles inland. From Willets, it was a straight shot to the posh community north of San Francisco called Highland Hills where Santi had retired several months before.

The rain finally let up as they crossed a bridge over a swollen stream. Their headlights picked out images of tumultuous water edging the bank. The current appeared voracious and matched the mood in the car, as did the high clouds racing across the sky, covering the moon and then revealing it like a lofty version of cat and mouse.

They passed a sign announcing thirty more miles before they would intersect the highway. Traffic was relatively light. Hannah's eyelids began involuntarily closing as the car ate up the miles and Jack concentrated on driving. A growling stomach kept her awake for a while, but soon even hunger couldn't dull the fatigue that scratched at her eyelids.

She awoke with a jerk, awake instantly, heart thumping wildly in her chest like a pinball machine gone berserk. "What is it?" she said, looking over at Jack.

Dashboard lights revealed his strong profile. He spared her a very quick glance. "There's a black van behind us. It's coming right up on our tailpipe and then backing down. Hold on."

That's what she'd felt, the jerkiness of his driving. They were traveling fast, the twists of the road following those of the river, forcing braking and wide turns. As she turned to look back, the headlamps behind them grew larger, flooding the car with light.

A black van. It finally sank in. "The van from the car park? Hugo?"

"Who else would do this?" he said, and this time the van came right up and touched the back bumper. The car lurched.

"Is your seat belt fastened?" Jack asked, his voice tight as once again the back bumper took a hit.

Hannah's mouth was too dry to speak. As if from an overhead viewpoint, she pictured the huge van bearing down on her tiny car like an agile, strong cheetah chasing down a half-grown gazelle. The fact was her belt wasn't fastened; she'd taken it off to tend to the baby and fallen asleep without redoing it. Now she felt around frantically for the loose end, but then she thought of Aubrielle's seat. Was it as tight as it could be? She leaned over the back, feeling around in the dark for the strap to cinch it. The van shot past them.

Jack yelled a warning just as the van careened into their lane, crashing Jack's side of the car, pushing Hannah's small vehicle off the pavement. They rushed at a thirty-degree angle into the trees on the side of the road. Branches whipped Hannah's side of the car as Jack fought the steering wheel. Hannah turned in time to catch a glimpse of the water beyond the trees, bathed in moonlight, silver on gray.

The car began sliding sideways down the steep bank toward the water, which slowed its forward motion. *Aubrielle*. If the car went into the water, the baby wouldn't survive the cold and dark. Hannah screamed at Jack, who was still struggling with steering. Hannah's door sprung open and she grabbed the seat back. Aubrielle began crying as the noise of metal pressing against rock and splintered trees surrounded them.

At last the car came to a tilted, rolling stop. Hannah

slipped toward her open door. Jack reached forward and grabbed her hand. "Hold on to me," he yelled as the car, groaning, slid some more. At least the engine was off. Hannah's legs flew free of the car. The river rushed over the rocks right below her. The car moved again and she slipped farther, Jack still holding on to her with a fierce grip.

"You have to get Aubrielle out the other side, Jack," she yelled.

"I won't let go of you—"

"You have to. It's her only chance."

"Hold on."

The car slipped a little more. Hannah's foot caught the water and it started dragging her. It was so black inside the car she couldn't see anything but the whites of Jack's eyes and the flash of his teeth.

"I'll—" Jack began, but she cut him off.

"Listen to me. You have to save Aubrielle. You have to get her out the high side of this car before it slides into the water. If the car goes in, we'll never get her out in time."

"You're all she has," he said firmly. "I can get you both—"

"No, you can't." The water dragged her more, her fingers slipped in his hand. "I'm not all she has," she gasped as a sob welled deep in her gut. "I'm not all, Jack. She has her father. She has you."

Her announcement was met with total silence as though both the man and the baby stopped breathing, stopped everything. Groaning, the car slipped yet again and so did Hannah's fingers from Jack's grasp. She tried to catch the door frame but the current was too strong. The river swept her away, water closing over her head, cold creeping steadily inward as she struggled to find the surface.

FOR ONE INTERMINABLE MOMENT, Jack stared at the dark water rushing by the car and the void where Hannah had been just seconds before.

And then he heard a cry from the backseat and everything came into focus. He moved carefully, willing the damn car to stay on the bank another few minutes. Reaching back, he felt around until he found the straps of the car seat and managed to release the clip that held the seat in place. Then he pulled the seat across the back until he could more or less scoop the crying infant out and get her across the back of the seat and into his arms. The diaper bag was caught on the shift knob and he pulled it free. At the last second, he remembered to pop the Beethoven tape out of the player and stick it in the diaper bag.

The car groaned and shifted. Water rushed by close enough to touch it. Water that had washed Hannah from his grip—no, he couldn't think about Hannah, he just had to get her baby out of this car.

Her baby. *His baby.* He'd always known it. Somewhere deep inside, in his heart. Now he also understood why he'd continued to feel Hannah was hiding something from him. She'd had no intention of telling him about being a father until things got so desperate she had to. She didn't trust him.

He held his crying daughter as tight as he could up high against his shoulder while he held his breath and pushed on the door that had been crunched when the van sideswiped him. Expecting his movements would send them into the water at any moment, he finally managed to inch the protesting metal ajar. Next he worked on getting one leg outside, one foot on the riverbank. Shifting his weight to that leg, he used his body to wedge himself free of the car, doing his best to protect Abby's fragile head. Finally free, he stumbled up the bank in an effort to put as much distance between himself and the car as possible.

With a metallic thump or two, the car continued its slide toward the river, its headlights illuminating the watery grave it would soon enter.

"Hey!" someone shouted from above. "Hey down there."

Jack was torn between relief and alarm. Had Hugo Correa come back for the kill? He looked down the river for some sign of Hannah, knowing it was unlikely he could see her even if she'd managed to escape the current as she was dressed in black.

"Is that a baby?" a woman's voice called.

A woman. Jack began scrambling up the bank as lights from above lit the ground before him. The minute he got to the top, he found himself facing an older couple. Their giant RV bus was pulled off the road behind them. They both held flashlights.

"Oh, my goodness," the woman cried. "It is a baby. I thought it was. Is she all right?"

"She's fine but I need help," Jack said quickly.

"My name is Jim Franklin. This is the wife, Caroline. What do you need?"

"The baby's mother is in the water. Take the baby, keep her warm, give me a flashlight."

"Sure, of course," the man said, as his wife exchanged her flashlight for Abby and the diaper bag.

"We don't have a phone that works out here but I'll come with you," Mr. Franklin said.

"No. You stay here with your wife," Jack insisted. He

was already moving off. He didn't want Abby and the woman alone if Hugo came back.

Turning away, he slipped and slid his way down the riverbank, his light playing out in front of him as he struggled to make his way through the brush. "Hannah," he called until his voice turned raspy. "Hannah, please, Hannah."

A few times he thought he saw her dark shape on the bank and he ran, slipping in the mud, but it was never her, it was always a rock or a piece of waterlogged wood. He climbed boulders to avoid having to travel away from the river's edge, pushing branches out of his way with increasingly scratched hands, calling her name again and again. When he couldn't avoid it, he waded through the water itself, unwilling to leave any patch of riverbank unchecked.

His light illuminated some large rocks poking out into the river, which would mean a steep climb, and his heart sank. Until now, the shore had been more or less navigable in the dark and had paralleled the road overhead, but here it appeared to turn one hundred and eighty degrees. He needed help.

Help meant law enforcement. Law enforcement meant possible incarceration. It meant time delays no one could afford, it meant losing Abby if the worst happened and Hannah was dead. He was trapped between a rock and a hard place and all he could think of was that if Hannah was to get a chance at all, what happened to him didn't matter. She mattered.

He shined the light on the bank in front of the rock formation and saw another patch of black. That's when he realized the twisting river might create a change in the current, might give someone struggling to get to the shore an opportunity to do so. Heart racing again, he yelled, "Hannah," and ran toward the dark shape.

His light picked up blondish hair and a surge of emotion seemed to fuel his limbs. The next thing he knew, he was falling to his knees with no knowledge of how he'd covered the remaining ground, falling to his knees beside Hannah.

"Cariño," he whispered as he turned her over, afraid he was too late....

Her skin was pale and cold to the touch. He felt her throat for a pulse and as he did so, she began coughing. He helped her turn to her stomach, where she was able to throw up the water that she'd swallowed until eventually she held her head in her hands.

"Are you all right?" he asked, taking off his coat and putting it around her shoulders.

"Aubrielle?" she mumbled.

"She's okay, she's safe." He kissed her cold lips and rubbed her hands between his. "Are you really all right?"

"Just tired...cold...wet," she stuttered.

"When I thought I'd lost you—" he began but stopped. There was a lot that needed to be said, but blurting things out after the scare they'd both just had and on the heels of her revelation seemed unwise. He didn't want to go making promises he couldn't keep to a woman who had waited until the last second to tell him something so vital.

A crashing sound on the bank above them caused them both to jump. "Stay still," Jack urged as he switched off the light. Once again he pictured Hugo, gun drawn, somehow hunting them down. Hannah was still shaky, she couldn't run and he wouldn't leave her. They were sitting ducks. He tried to shield her.

"Did you find her?" a man called and with infinite relief, Jack recognized Jim Franklin's voice. The older guy appeared on the ledge above them, his blinding light momentarily playing over them. "Is she okay?"

"Yes," Jack rasped.

"Caroline and I have been following your light along the river. The RV is right up the hill."

"Who in the world is that?" Hannah mumbled through trembling lips as Jack helped her to her feet.

"Guardian angels," he said. "Let's go."

HANNAH, DRESSED IN JEANS AND a bulky sweater loaned to her by Caroline Franklin, held her baby tight in her arms. There was no better therapy for what she'd been through than to sit close to Jack and hold Aubrielle.

She'd almost lost everything tonight. Only the last little bit of fight left in her body had set off an alarm when the currents began to change and she'd paddled weak as a kitten to shore, crawling up on the rocks, not knowing if she was really alive or lying on the bank of eternity.

Not until Jack lifted her in his arms.

"So when we got rained out on the coast, we decided to drive inland to go visit our son and his family," Caroline said. "They live in San Rafael."

The bus was just entering Willets, Jim behind the wheel. "Sign says police up ahead," he shouted. "That's where I'll take you unless you want to go directly to the hospital."

Hannah slid a glance at Jack, who looked ready to jump out of his skin. "Do you think you could take us all the way to Highland Hills?" she asked.

"What about your car?" the man said, glancing over his shoulder. "And don't you need to see a doctor?"

"No, no doctor. We're in a terrible hurry to get to Highland Hills, we'll worry about the car tomorrow." There were a lot of things Hannah would worry about tomorrow such as what she'd set in motion when she'd confessed Jack was Aubrielle's father. Just look at the way he avoided looking at her.

"We could do that," the woman said, tucking curly gray hair behind her ears. She had a round, pleasant face, full of kindness. "It's right on the way to our son's place."

"You can just let us off in town and we could get a cab," Jack said.

"Don't be silly," the man called. "We'll take you where you need to go. No problem."

HANNAH HAD NEVER BEEN TO Santi Correa's house before, but she'd forwarded enough mail the last few months to have the address down pat. The Franklins drove them right up to the gated driveway where Jack asked they hang around for a few minutes.

"Call Santi on the intercom," he coached, "and make sure Hugo didn't get here before us."

"The last person in the world Hugo would come to after what he's done is his father."

"Both the shotgun and rifle were in the truck when your car slid into the river. We're unarmed. Humor me."

Holding Aubrielle, Hannah punched the call button on the intercom. Santi responded at once. "You're here at last," he said, relief in his voice. "I was getting worried."

"I'm sorry we're late," Hannah said. Jack had pointed out the camera atop the gate and had stepped into the shadows before she initiated the call. She added, "Will we have complete privacy?"

He chuckled. "It's almost midnight, sweetheart. My wife is asleep, the staff have left for the day. Where's your car?"

"I'll explain. Will you let us in?"

"Yes, yes, of course." The latch on a pedestrian gate next to the driveway clicked on as lights illuminated a path.

They waved the Franklins off with their profuse thanks and started down the path. The bruises Hannah had acquired on her trip down the river took a backseat to her nerves. The situation wasn't helped when Jack, leaning close to whisper, said, "Hugo could still show up, things could take a bad turn. Stay alert."

Chapter Fifteen

Santi answered the door.

"Hannah, my dear girl," he said, opening the door wide. White brows arched over dark eyes as his gaze moved on to Jack, then narrowed as though trying to place him.

"This is my friend, Jack Starling," Hannah said. "You met him a year ago in Tierra Montañosa."

Jack held out a hand and Santi shook it, his grip stronger than Jack had expected given what Hannah had said about his frail condition. He was getting older, sure, his shoulders more slumped, his hair whiter, but there was still fire in the old guy's eyes.

"Dias bueno, mi amigo," Santi said. "What miracle is this? We all thought you had perished in the jungle."

"I was lucky, sir," Jack said. "But tonight we come with some alarming news that concerns Tierra Montañosa."

"Come inside, come inside," Santi said, closing the door behind them. "Please, if you don't mind my saying so, you both look as though you've had a rough trip. Come into the den, let me make you a drink." He led the way into a lofty room containing a glass desk at one end and a gathering of chairs at the other, a majestic marble fireplace a focal point for all. Santi carefully closed the tall gilt doors isolating the room from the rest of the house. "I haven't met your baby yet, Hannah," he said with a wistful smile. "Her name is Aubrielle, isn't that right?"

Hannah lowered the baby from her shoulder to show Santi Abby's face. Santi said, "She's as lovely as her mother. May I hold her?"

Hannah paused for a second and then said, "Of course."

"Let me sit in this chair. I'm an old man. I wouldn't want to drop her." Hannah gently placed the bundled baby in his lap.

He smiled warmly. "Jack, will you do the honors? I'll have whiskey and water."

"I'll have the same," Hannah said softly.

Jack poured straight whiskey for himself and handed out the drinks. Choosing a chair across from Santi, he wondered where they should start. With an explanation, with the tape?

Hannah looked at him and then at her hands and then at Santi before saying, "We've come to talk to you about Hugo."

"Hugo? What does Hugo have to do with Tierra Montañosa? The schools there are open, the foundation is working on schools in Colombia now."

"But it is about the schools," Hannah said, casting Jack a pleading look. "And the ambush and the GTM—"

"Sir, do you have an audio tape player?" Jack interrupted. "It may save a lot of time."

Santi looked surprised by the request, then shrugged indulgently as though humoring him. "In the cabinet. It's part of an old system I like too much to replace." He gestured at the large oak armoire against the wall. Jack dug in Hannah's diaper bag and withdrew David's tape. After fiddling with the machine, David's voice filled the room. "April 30, 11:20 a.m., Correa and Hurtado, Tierra Montañosa border, aboard Bell charter N480EX."

"What is this?" Santi snapped, leaning forward over Aubrielle. "Who is this man Hurtado?"

"Just listen," Jack said.

The Spanish conversation caught Santi's attention. Cradling Abby, he leaned forward and listened. Once again, Jack heard Correa and Hurtado make plans to drug Jack, make plans for the ambush and the bogus press releases intended to mislead everyone into thinking they were dealing with the GTM.

"You were drugged?" Santi said when it finally wound down.

"Yes," Jack said, crossing to turn off Beethoven's ninth, which had resumed playing. "That's why I wasn't in the lead car. I don't think I was supposed to show up at all, but in the end I did and was captured."

"But you weren't killed. They said they would kill anyone the insurance company wouldn't ransom."

"Yes, but I think they decided they could turn me into one of them. They were training marksmen and I have skills in that area. Hugo must have known about me. I guess anyone at Staar would have had access to my résumé."

Santi got to his feet, Abby held gently in his arms. He walked to his desk and touched the phone. Jack was relieved he was going into action so promptly, but then Santi put the phone down and took a few steps toward the doors, paused, turned and looked back at them. "You are accusing my son of murder. Worse, terrorism."

"And that's not all," Jack said. "Don't forget the

end, don't forget they mentioned something about the thirtieth anniversary."

"You think they meant the Founder's Day open house."

"What else?"

"Hmm—"

"Listen, I saw them practicing down there, setting up mock attacks. I don't know how they'd get here and how they could disappear in a community as small as Fort Bragg, but they must have a plan and your son must be facilitating it. For all we know there could be others on the staff—"

"This is sounding slightly insane, you know that," Santi said. His voice sounded stronger, the set of his shoulders more square.

"Maybe I am," Jack said, "But you don't know what's been going on during your absence, especially the last few days."

Santi brushed that aside. "Who else knows of this tape?" Santi asked.

"Just your son," Hannah said. "The man who made it was David Lengell and as you know, he died right afterward. He was blackmailing Hugo."

Santi shook his white head.

"I know this is a lot to swallow all at once," Hannah said. "We can explain more later. For now, please, just cancel Sunday's events. You're the only one with the necessary power to cut through the red tape. Your son tried to kill us tonight. He needs to be stopped."

A knock on the door caused Santi to turn on his heels. He walked to the door and opened one slender panel. Hugo Correa entered, visibly shaken when he got a good look at his father's visitors.

"Ah, Hugo, yes, thank you for answering my summons. We have guests."

Hugo looked terrible, worse, if possible, than he had in the guerilla camp months before. There was a wild abandon evident in his eyes, salt-and-pepper hair flopped over his forehead, and his round face had an unhealthy sheen. As he limped into the room, his eyes burned with malice directed at Hannah. Even his clothes looked like rejects from a secondhand store, though the tailored gray suit had probably cost a bundle.

So Santi had lied about his son not being here. Maybe he'd been trying to protect him. Jack could understand the impulse, but the time had come and gone for looking the other way. When he touched the phone, he must have pushed a button alerting Hugo and now here they all were. Damn.

Hannah seemed to shrink in her chair. Her gaze went to Santi before dropping to her baby whom Santi still held.

"You," Hugo said, pointing a shaky finger at Hannah. "Why couldn't you just give me the tape?"

"Why should I?" she said with a defiant tilt of her chin. "You've been terrorizing me. You could have killed my baby." She slid Jack a glance as though realizing she'd just remembered telling him Abby was his child, as well.

"What does what happened ten years ago matter now? Why would you try to ruin the foundation because of that? How much money—"

"I don't know what you're talking about," she said.

"Like hell you don't."

"What *are* you talking about?" Jack said, getting to his feet, fists balled at his sides. Santi might be willing to stand there and watch, but Jack wasn't.

"You've been blackmailing my father," Hugo said, his gaze never straying from Hannah. "You've been bleeding him dry and then even though he paid you, you threatened to go public. Did you kill Fran, too? Did she find out about you?"

"Okay, you've completely lost me," Hannah said. "I have never blackmailed anybody."

"You deny you sent me an e-mail this afternoon? And one to my father?" Hugo demanded as Santi recrossed the room, coming to a stop in front of the big marble fireplace where a fire blazed in the grate.

"No, I don't deny it but that was just to flush you out because you took my baby and threatened to kill her and my grandmother—"

"I never," he said, stepping back, hand at his throat. His eyes were suddenly as confused as Hannah's.

"You ran us off the road tonight," Jack said.

"Yes, yes, I was crazy trying to keep you from going to the newspapers with the sex tape of my father and that lobbyist. I knew you were going to give a press conference that would start a state investigation. He had no idea that woman was using him, getting him into compromising situations. I shouldn't have pulled a gun in the car park, either, I admit that. I was frantic."

"You almost killed Hannah and Abby," Jack said through clenched teeth.

Hannah said, "Wait a second. I don't know anything about a sex tape. You broke into my home, you bombed my car, you plotted with terrorists to kill your own employees—"

Now it was Hugo's turn to throw up his hands. "You lie," he said. "I never did any of those things. I hired a private eye, but he insisted he wouldn't break any laws. All he did was keep track of your movements."

"Are you saying you didn't plot the ambush with a man named Hurtado, that you didn't scheme to form some kind of bogus GTM group, that you didn't kill David and Fran or plan some kind of massacre for the open house—"

Hugo's mouth literally dropped open. "What about the open house?"

"There's a plan to sabotage it and blame it on terrorists," she said. "As if you didn't know."

"They're coming here? That's nuts. If they wanted to do something like that, they'd attack their own schools. The foundation schools are having festivities, too, lots of community leaders and government officials. A lot easier to create chaos close to home than here. What would be the point? How could they all even get into the States?"

A deep silence fell over the room and Jack, who had been allowing his emotions to get the better of him, finally took a second to use his brain.

Hurtado and Correa.

Which Correa?

He looked at Santi, who was holding Abby out in front of him. Her blanket had fallen away and she lay in his hands, on her back, sound asleep, tiny and so fragile you could almost see her pulse throb in her temple.

His child. His future. Jack took a step.

"That's enough," Santi said.

Hannah rose in one fluid motion as though she sensed the shift in the air just as Jack had.

"Isn't it amazing how delicate a baby is," Santi said, staring at Abby. "Any child, really. Not just babies. Any child. And we lose so many of them."

"Mr. Correa?" Hannah said, advancing slowly. "I'd like my baby back."

He glanced at her. "Stay there, my dear. You have it all wrong. My son doesn't have the guts to do what you've accused him of doing. It's amazing to me he had the nerve to run you off the road tonight. Maybe there's hope for him, after all."

"I don't understand," Hannah said.

Jack inched forward a little, and spoke. "It wasn't Hugo on the tape, it was Santi. I couldn't tell their voices apart because the sound quality was so poor."

"What tape?" Hugo said. "The sex tape?"

"There probably is no sex tape," Jack said. "Your father has been using you, Hugo. He sold you down the creek. The tape he wanted was a recording made in Tierra Montañosa by David Lengell. So, Santi, where is Mitch Reynolds? You hired him to kill David after David extorted the first fifty thousand. Then Mitch started terrorizing Hannah because Fran took over where David left off and blamed it on Hannah. Did Mitch kill Fran for you, too?"

Santi shrugged. "She got greedy and stupid and revealed her identity. Hannah, I tried to spare. She was a mother, after all. But Fran…" He shook his head in distaste and added, "After Mitch Reynolds took care of that meddlesome private investigator who was always showing up at the wrong time, I thought it wise he take an extended vacation."

"I don't understand," Hugo said. "Why are they saying these things about you, Dad?"

Jack, staring at Santi, who still had total control over Abby, made a leap. "It's the schools. That's what the thirtieth anniversary remarks pertained to. It's not the foundation that's the target, it's one of the schools, just as you suggested, Hugo."

"Very good," Santi said with a smile. "But you think too small."

"It's all of the schools."

"Just those in Tierra Montañosa."

"But why would you fund a group pretending to be the GTM?" Hugo asked. It appeared he was fighting the depth of his father's depravity, circling it like a wary dog, poking at it. "Why would you destroy what you've spent your life and most of mine creating? Those schools are beautiful."

"The schools are buildings," Santi said. "I'm not interested in the buildings."

Jack thought of the mock attacks he'd witnessed. The snipers in the jungle picking off imaginary targets—visiting dignitaries brought to the schools to make speeches? He thought of the school bus he'd seen in camp one day. Many of the guerillas had boarded and left in it. He'd thought at the time it was troop movement, but now another conclusion demanded attention. Maybe it had been part of the setup. Maybe the guerillas would arrive in buses...

Beside him, Hannah took another step toward Santi. "Give me my baby," she said firmly. Jack took the opportunity to move closer, as well. Santi pulled Abby back against his chest. The baby woke up with a squawk, close to crying.

"One more step and I drop her on the marble. Her head will split open like a ripe melon, Hannah. She is just one child, no more important than the hundreds like her who will die tomorrow."

Hannah froze.

"You're going to kill the children," Jack said, shocked.

"That's not possible," Hugo said, but the horror in his eyes suggested he was finally catching on.

"Year after year we build schools and the children come but eventually, the GTM or groups like them take the children away," Santi said. "Girls and boys both are lured into the jungle to carry guns or work in the drug trade to finance the very terrorism the citizens are too apathetic to stop. It will never end."

"So you created bogus rebels to do an unspeakable act of terrorism that will what? Galvanize the populace?" Jack asked.

"The mass slaughter of children, teachers and leaders with the GTM taking credit for it, flaunting it even, will outrage the population in a way the silent cries of the innocent does not. The people will finally demand their government crack down on the GTM and the drug trade that corrupts everything on every level. A few lives spent now will see many saved down the line."

"This kind of thing never works," Jack said. "Zealots like you all over the world try to force their views on people and it never works."

"But I have right on my side," Santi said. "This will go down in history as the day that started a new movement in Tierra Montañosa. No one will ever know I was behind it and that's okay. It will be my true legacy."

Hugo stepped closer to his father. "You arranged the ambush?"

"Yes, yes, of course," Santi said as though bored with the topic. "Me and Hurtado."

If Jack had been armed, he could have taken Santi out in a single shot. The old man would never have known what hit him. The danger would be for Abby, of course. She was far too young to survive a fall to that unforgiving rock. As he wasn't armed this was all academic, but his fingers still itched with the desire to pull a trigger and end this lunacy.

All four adults stood in a circle, all facing one another, cords of tension radiating between them. Jack's mind raced as he desperately tried to come up with a plan.

Hugo said, "You weren't sick that night in the hotel. You pretended you were so I'd insist you stay behind. You knew those killers were going to come and you sent me and the others."

Santi's upper lip curled. "Have you always been so dense?"

"I spent weeks with those monsters. I thought I was going to die. They shot me. And you let them."

"The shot was necessary," Santi said complacently, "to make sure no one suspected the foundation of collusion. We needed capital. I figured we'd get you back."

"You were dispensable," Jack said, deciding that feeding Hugo's sense of betrayal might work for them. "You were no more important to him that anyone else."

"That's not true," Santi said. "My son was worth several million dollars."

Hannah reached out a hand. "Mr. Correa, Santi. It's over. Give me Aubrielle. There's nowhere to go now, too many people know about this. Give me my baby, please."

"I'll tell you what we're going to do," Santi said. "We're all going to wait. The festivities in Tierra Montañosa are on Saturday. Sunday is a holy day and they insisted they celebrate a day early. The ambush will take place at all three schools simultaneously beginning at nine in the morning. They're three hours ahead of us there, so at six tomorrow morning, it will begin. I will give you your baby at six-thirty."

"And then we'll tell the media what you've done and the GTM will not be blamed and all your grandiose plans will go up in smoke," Jack said.

"You make a good point," Santi said. "I have been working toward this one event with blinders on, but you're right. Your survival will ruin everything." He looked at Hannah and added, "You have my word I'll see to it your grandmother gets your baby to raise."

Before Hannah could throw herself on the old man, Hugo produced a .38 Special. Santi saw it and smiled. "I don't expect you to turn into a man tonight, son. You don't have to shoot anyone. Mitch has been doing my dirty work, but I'm not above taking care of these two myself."

"I'm not pointing it at them," Hugo said. "I'm pointing it at you."

Santi chuckled. "Even if you were able to kill me, which I highly doubt, you'd probably also kill this innocent child."

"You're willing to sacrifice hundreds to save millions," Hugo said calmly. "Perhaps I'm willing to sacrifice one to save those hundreds."

"No, no, you'll hit Aubrielle," Hannah cried as Santi held Abby against his chest.

"Don't worry, Hannah. He doesn't have the guts," Santi said, his voice complacent.

For a second, Jack thought Santi was right, but something snapped in Hugo's eyes and his gun hand straightened.

Pushing Hannah to the floor, Jack dove for Santi as the gun went off.

Chapter Sixteen

Hannah rolled over at once, twisting as gunfire echoed in the small enclosed room. She was in time to see Aubrielle falling one direction as Santi fell another. Jack slid along the floor, arms stretched out in front, gaze totally focused on the baby.

Everything switched to slow motion. The baby fell in millimeters as Jack's hands inched above his head. Hannah stopped breathing and was hardly aware of Santi's body crumbled on the marble, her concentration riveted on the two people she loved most in the world.

Jack caught Aubrielle in his strong, tan hands and the film sped, time went back to normal speed. She was on her feet and beside them without pausing to think, taking the baby from Jack, hugging the squalling infant close as Jack sat up and grinned at her.

Hugo walked over to his father's desk and sat down heavily, laying the pistol on the glass top with a clatter.

Jack sprang to his feet, took one of Hannah's hands to help her stand. Holding the baby close, she paced the room, jiggling Aubrielle, trying to calm her. There were blood splatters on her sleeper, but none had touched her skin.

Jack walked over to Santi's body. Leaning down, he

touched the old guy's papery throat and met Hannah's gaze. He shook his head.

Hugo moaned. "I killed my father," he said, and stiffly picked up the receiver.

"Call off the Tierra Montañosa celebrations before you call the police," Jack said.

"I can't. I have to report—"

Jack reached Hugo in two strides and took the receiver. "If you call the police first, you may not get the opportunity to call Tierra Montañosa in time. Call them first. Insist they act right now. They need to call in police and media, they need to stop this, they need to find the local contact, a man named Hurtado. They only have a few hours."

"But the law says—"

"Hugo? Your father is dead, you did what you had to do. A few more minutes aren't going to matter. Finish what you started."

Hugo gulped and nodded. As he searched for an address book, Jack walked back to Hannah. She'd finally managed to calm Aubrielle to the point where her cries had evolved into hiccups.

Jack put his hands around her upper arms and, leaning down, kissed her forehead, then he leaned farther and kissed Aubrielle. Tears burned the back of her throat as she watched him.

"You saved her," she said.

"Well, I am her bodyguard."

"And her father."

"About that—"

"Jack, I'm sorry I told you the way I did." As Hugo's Spanish grew increasingly fevered in the background, she tried to express her feelings accurately. "Please don't think I expect you to change your whole life because of one night with me and the baby we created. I hope you'll be a part of her life, but—"

"Shut up," he said softly, gazing into her eyes.

"Shut up?"

"You told me I was her father when you thought there was no other choice and not a minute sooner. You didn't trust me. You lied to me. If you hadn't thought your death was imminent, you never would have told me."

How did she argue any of that when it was all true? He hated her; he had every right. "I wanted to tell you but I was afraid," she mumbled.

"Afraid of what?"

"That you wouldn't want her," she said. "Or that you'd want her too much."

"Hannah, what were you *really* afraid of?"

His question startled her. She blinked a couple of times and swallowed tears. She thought of hedging, thought of turning away, thought of losing him forever. "I was afraid you wouldn't want...us," she finally murmured.

He lowered his head and rested his cheek against her forehead. "You barely knew me," he whispered.

"But I loved you," she said, and it was as though the steel bands holding her heart together sprang apart. But it was true and he might as well know it.

He cupped her face with his warm hand. "And that's why I came looking for you, too, *cariño*. Because I loved you."

She buried her head against his chest as all the tension of the last twenty-four hours drained away, dissolving her bones in the process. She was limp and exhausted and suddenly hungry beyond enduring.

He loved her. She looked up at his face and said, "So you won't be driving off on your Harley?"

"Who, me?" he said, his fingers now caressing Aubrielle's cheek. "I don't own a Harley anymore. I just own a truck you tried to kill this afternoon. Besides, I have responsibilities. I'm a family man now. I guess I should ask. Hannah, will you marry me?"

Smiling, she nodded.

Epilogue

Six Months Later

Snow fell gently as Jack pulled into Simon and Ella's driveway. He'd been to Blue Mountain only once, many months before, right after they'd all returned from Canada. At the time, he'd been fresh from the jungle, driven to find out what had happened to him and why, and positive the former Hannah Marks had had something to do with it.

And now she sat beside him, his wife of two weeks, the love of his life. "I hope they like me," she said.

He took her hand, raised it to his lips and kissed her knuckles. "How could they not love you?" he asked.

"You may be prejudiced."

"You can count on that."

A squawk from the backseat announced the baby had had enough sitting and driving and wanted out of the car. They obliged her. Jack's arms were full of presents as Hannah rang the bell of the gray house with the white shutters and the bright red door.

It had taken him months to settle the legal issues caused by reentering the country the way he had, months that had also seen the collapse of the Staar Foundation. He and Hannah had married quietly, privately, after everything was finally settled. They'd recently moved to a larger city with more opportunities and he was working on getting his private investigator license. They spent many weekends with Mimi and, simply put, life had never been so good.

The door opened and Ella stood there, her hair longer now. Her eyes widened when she got a look at Hannah and their nine-month-old baby who was a dead ringer for Jack.

"*This* is your surprise," Ella said, laughing and reaching out to hug Hannah.

"This is my wife, Hannah," Jack said and completed the introductions.

"Come in, come in," Ella said, stepping aside. Over her shoulder, she called, "Simon? Come here. Wait until you see Jack's big surprise."

As they stepped inside the house, the smell of roasting turkey, the twinkle of Christmas lights, the sound of the "Hallelujah Chorus" playing on the stereo lifted Jack's heart in a way he still wasn't used to. Could this beautiful woman with this charming home and family really be his little sister? Could she have actually traveled so far from the sadness of her past?

Why not? He had.

Simon entered from the hall, their newborn in his arms. He grinned when he saw Jack and then he saw Hannah and his eyes lit up. "I am so glad to meet you," he said, handing his daughter to Ella so he could hug Hannah. "Jack, you scoundrel, you kept these two beauties a secret? You've got some explaining to do."

"We wanted to surprise you," Jack said. "There's been a lot going on, a lot to talk about."

"I'll pour the wine," Simon said, but he paused to put

an arm around Ella. "What's your little girl's name?" he asked.

Hannah said, "Abby."

At the same moment Jack said, "Aubrielle."

And they smiled at each other.

* * * * *

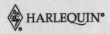 HARLEQUIN®

INTRIGUE

COMING NEXT MONTH

Available July 13, 2010

HICNM0610

REQUEST YOUR FREE BOOKS!

2 FREE NOVELS
PLUS 2
FREE GIFTS!

HARLEQUIN®

INTRIGUE®

Breathtaking Romantic Suspense

YES! Please send me 2 FREE Harlequin Intrigue® novels and my 2 FREE gifts (gifts are worth about $10). After receiving them, if I don't wish to receive any more books, I can return the shipping statement marked "cancel." If I don't cancel, I will receive 6 brand-new novels every month and be billed just $4.24 per book in the U.S. or $4.99 per book in Canada. That's a saving of at least 15% off the cover price! It's quite a bargain! Shipping and handling is just 50¢ per book.* I understand that accepting the 2 free books and gifts places me under no obligation to buy anything. I can always return a shipment and cancel at any time. Even if I never buy another book from Harlequin, the two free books and gifts are mine to keep forever.

182/382 HDN E5MG

Name   (PLEASE PRINT)

Address   Apt. #

City   State/Prov.   Zip/Postal Code

Signature (if under 18, a parent or guardian must sign)

Mail to the Harlequin Reader Service:
IN U.S.A.: P.O. Box 1867, Buffalo, NY 14240-1867
IN CANADA: P.O. Box 609, Fort Erie, Ontario L2A 5X3
Not valid for current subscribers to Harlequin Intrigue books.

**Are you a subscriber to Harlequin Intrigue books and
want to receive the larger-print edition? Call 1-800-873-8635 today!**

* Terms and prices subject to change without notice. Prices do not include applicable taxes. N.Y. residents add applicable sales tax. Canadian residents will be charged applicable provincial taxes and GST. Offer not valid in Quebec. This offer is limited to one order per household. All orders subject to approval. Credit or debit balances in a customer's account(s) may be offset by any other outstanding balance owed by or to the customer. Please allow 4 to 6 weeks for delivery. Offer available while quantities last.

Your Privacy: Harlequin is committed to protecting your privacy. Our Privacy Policy is available online at www.eHarlequin.com or upon request from the Reader Service. From time to time we make our lists of customers available to reputable third parties who may have a product or service of interest to you. If you would prefer we not share your name and address, please check here. ☐

Help us get it right—We strive for accurate, respectful and relevant communications. To clarify or modify your communication preferences, visit us at www.ReaderService.com/consumerschoice.

HI10R

HARLEQUIN®

A Romance

FOR EVERY MOOD™

Spotlight on
Heart & Home

Heartwarming romances
where love can happen
right when you least expect it.

See the next page to enjoy a sneak peek
from Silhouette Special Edition®,
a Heart and Home series.

*Introducing McFARLANE'S PERFECT BRIDE
by USA TODAY bestselling author Christine Rimmer,
from Silhouette Special Edition®.*

Entranced. Captivated. Enchanted.

Connor sat across the table from Tori Jones and couldn't help thinking that those words exactly described what effect the small-town schoolteacher had on him. He might as well stop trying to tell himself he wasn't interested. He was powerfully drawn to her.

Clearly, he should have dated more when he was younger.

There had been a couple of other women since Jennifer had walked out on him. But he had never been entranced. Or captivated. Or enchanted.

Until now.

He wanted her—*her,* Tori Jones, in particular. Not just someone suitably attractive and well-bred, as Jennifer had been. Not just someone sophisticated, sexually exciting and discreet, which pretty much described the two women he'd dated after his marriage crashed and burned.

It came to him that he…he *liked* this woman. And that was new to him. He liked her quick wit, her wisdom and her big heart. He liked the passion in her voice when she talked about things she believed in.

He liked *her.* And suddenly it mattered all out of proportion that she might like him, too.

Was he losing it? He couldn't help but wonder. Was he cracking under the strain—of the soured economy, the McFarlane House setbacks, his divorce, the scary changes in his son? Of the changes he'd decided he needed to make in his life and himself?

Strangely, right then, on his first date with Tori Jones, he didn't care if he just might be going over the edge. He was having a great time—having *fun*, of all things—and he didn't want it to end.

Is Connor finally able to admit his feelings to Tori, and are they reciprocated?
Find out in McFARLANE'S PERFECT BRIDE
by USA TODAY *bestselling author Christine Rimmer.*
Available July 2010,
only from Silhouette Special Edition®.

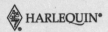

HARLEQUIN®
INTRIGUE®

**BESTSELLING
HARLEQUIN INTRIGUE AUTHOR**

DEBRA WEBB

**INTRODUCES THE LATEST
COLBY AGENCY SPIN-OFF**

No one or nothing would stand in the way
of an Equalizer agent…but every Colby agent
is a force to be reckoned with.

Look for

COLBY CONTROL—*July*
COLBY VELOCITY—*August*

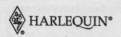
HARLEQUIN®

Showcase

LESLIE KELLY
Naturally Naughty

Wicked & Willing

On sale June 8

Reader favorites from the most talented voices in romance

Save $1.00 on the purchase of 1 or more Harlequin® Showcase books.

SAVE $1.00 on the purchase of 1 or more Harlequin® Showcase books.

Coupon expires November 30, 2010. Redeemable at participating retail outlets. Limit one coupon per customer. Valid in the U.S.A. and Canada only.

52609057

Canadian Retailers: Harlequin Enterprises Limited will pay the face value of this coupon plus 10.25¢ if submitted by customer for this product only. Any other use constitutes fraud. Coupon is nonassignable. Void if taxed, prohibited or restricted by law. Consumer must pay any government taxes. Void if copied. Nielsen Clearing House ("NCH") customers submit coupons and proof of sales to Harlequin Enterprises Limited, P.O. Box 3000, Saint John, NB E2L 4L3, Canada. Non-NCH retailer—for reimbursement submit coupons and proof of sales directly to Harlequin Enterprises Limited, Retail Marketing Department, 225 Duncan Mill Rd., Don Mills, ON M3B 3K9, Canada.

5 65373 00076 2   (8100)0 11654

U.S. Retailers: Harlequin Enterprises Limited will pay the face value of this coupon plus 8¢ if submitted by customer for this product only. Any other use constitutes fraud. Coupon is nonassignable. Void if taxed, prohibited or restricted by law. Consumer must pay any government taxes. Void if copied. For reimbursement submit coupons and proof of sales directly to Harlequin Enterprises Limited, P.O. Box 880478, El Paso, TX 88588-0478, U.S.A. Cash value 1/100 cents.

® and TM are trademarks owned and used by the trademark owner and/or its licensee.
© 2010 Harlequin Enterprises Limited

HSCCOUP0610